ENVY

YURI OLESHA (1899–1960), the son of an impoverished land-owner who spent his days playing cards, grew up in Odessa, a lively multicultural city whose literary scene also included Isaac Babel. Olesha made his name as a writer with *Three Fat Men*, a proletarian fairy tale, and had an even greater success with *Envy* in 1927. Soon, however, the ambiguous nature of the novella's depiction of the new revolutionary era led to complaints from high, followed by the collapse of his career and the disappearance of his books. In 1934, Olesha addressed the First Congress of Soviet Writers, arguing that a writer should be allowed the freedom to choose his own style and themes. For the rest of his life he wrote very little. A memoir of his youth, *No Day Without a Line*, appeared posthumously.

KEN KALFUS's most recent book is a novel, *The Commissariat of Enlightenment*. He is also the author of two short story collections, *Thirst* and *Pu-239 and Other Russian Fantasies*.

ЗА
ВИ
СТЬ

РОМАН

юрий Олеша

ENVY

YURI OLESHA

Translated from the Russian by
MARIAN SCHWARTZ

Introduction by
KEN KALFUS

Illustrations by
NATAN ALTMAN

NEW YORK REVIEW BOOKS

New York

This is a New York Review Book
Published by The New York Review of Books
435 Hudson Street, New York, NY 10014
www.nyrb.com

Published by arrangement with FTM Agency, Ltd., Russia

Library of Congress Cataloging-in-Publication Data
Olesha, IUrii Karlovich, 1899–1960.
 [Zavist'. English]
 Envy / Yuri Olesha ; translated from the Russian by Marian Schwartz ; introduction
by Ken Kalfus.
     p. cm. — (New York Review Books classics)
 ISBN 1-59017-086-5 (pbk. : alk. paper)
 I. Schwartz, Marian. II. Title. III. Series.
 PG3476.O37Z213 2004
 891.73'42—dc22
                              2004004060

ISBN 978-1-59017-086-1

Printed in the United States of America on acid-free paper.
10 9 8 7 6 5

CONTENTS

INTRODUCTION · vii

PART ONE · 3

PART TWO · 75

INTRODUCTION

YURI OLESHA'S short novel *Envy* first appeared in the Soviet literary magazine *Red Virgin Soil* in the latter part of 1927, a perilous season in the history of the socialist republic. As Stalin consolidated power, the Party-controlled press warned of military intervention by Great Britain and its anti-Communist allies. The liberal New Economic Program was terminated, diminishing the supplies of produce and goods to the cities. The regime intensified its propaganda efforts. Bolshevik critics lashed out at the artistic avant-garde, which had flourished earlier in the decade. Late that autumn Stalin would crush the opposition at the 15th Party Congress and expel Trotsky from the Party—and fire the editor of *Red Virgin Soil*, Aleksandr Voronsky. After that, creative momentum would keep nonconformist artists in heedless motion for a few more years until they ran smack, sometimes fatally, into the wall of Party-dictated socialist realism.

We can imagine that summer of 1927 as having been very fine in Moscow, as "bright and breezy" as the day of the soccer match that occupies several chapters at the novel's conclusion. Food and other necessities were in short supply, but privations might have weighed gently on the shoulders of an up-and-coming, nondoctrinaire, twenty-eight-year-old writer on the staff of the *Whistle*, the widely read newspaper of the Railway Workers' Union. It was an illustrious staff: Olesha shared pages with Mikhail Bulgakov and his fellow Odessans Isaac Babel, Ilya Ilf, and Yevgeny Petrov. If they had managed to ignore day-to-day politics, they might have thought the Revolution could still tolerate satire and literary adventure.

In his work at the *Whistle*, Olesha found plenty of satirical targets among the low-level officials he held responsible for the quotidian incompetencies and indignities that plagued Soviet life (without implicating Party leaders, who were presumed to be struggling against them as well). He turned the familiarly knavish caricature on its head when he created *Envy*'s Andrei Babichev, the trade director of the Food Industry Trust, as a good-natured, happily corpulent, go-getting apparatchik. Andrei has devised a thirty-five-kopek sausage and intends to build a giant communal dining hall, to be called the Two Bits. These laughably materialistic projects, echoing Bolshevik promises reported in papers like the *Whistle*, become facets in a many-sided farce that obliquely sends up early Soviet mores and ambitions while speaking beyond Soviet borders on behalf of the individual conscience in a mechanizing, incorporating twentieth century.

Olesha's Andrei would be an unreservedly positive figure if his image were not mediated through the eyes of Nikolai Kavalerov, the spiteful young intellectual whom Andrei has rescued after finding him drunk in the street. The apparatchik has taken him back to his flat and generously installed him on the divan in his living room. From this vantage during the next several weeks, the wretched, self-loathing Nikolai observes Andrei's gross habits and intimate human failings— most damning of which is apparently the mole on his back. Nikolai bitterly envies Andrei's professional success and mocks the optimism of the Revolution. His enmity is stoked by the insults he imagines Andrei would hurl at *him* if the blameless Andrei were in fact to insult him.

Nikolai's black fantasies drive this novel, give it its avant-garde weirdness, and frustrate readers looking for a direct political interpretation. *Envy*'s most vivid scenes and dialogues don't actually occur—Nikolai invents them. For example when Andrei goes to a communal apartment house on an official visit, he's expelled by housewives angry at their domestic conditions. He leaves speechless. "He has no imagination." It's Nikolai who derisively tells the reader (not Andrei) that Andrei should have used that moment to promote the Two Bits. He supplies Andrei's putative and absurdly propagandistic exhortations:

> You, young wife, you cook your husband soup. You sacrifice half your day to a puddle of soup! We're going to transform your puddles into shimmering seas, we're going to ladle out cabbage soup by the ocean, pour kasha by the wheelbarrow, the blancmange is going to advance like a glacier! Listen, housewives, wait, this is what we're promising you: the tile floor bathed in sunlight, the copper kettles burnished, the saucers lily-white, the milk as heavy as quicksilver, and the smells rising from the soup so heavenly they'll be the envy of the flowers on your tables.

Nikolai renders (through Olesha; through the well-tuned lyricism of translator Marian Schwartz) this radiant future more memorably than he does the grim present. Time and again we see and don't see the real Andrei; we're confused by Nikolai's sarcastic mutterings that distort what the trade director has done and said, inflating his grandeur as well as his six-pood carnality. The image of Andrei Babichev is deliberately refracted through the prism of propaganda and the newly Sovietized Russian language, meant to accommodate revolutionary politics and the new communal and mechanized way of life. The result brings to mind the fractured and reflected human figures within early-twentieth-century Russian paintings like Pavel Filonov's *Victory over Eternity* and Kasimir Malevich's pre-war cubist masterpiece, *The Knife Grinder*.

Olesha further disorients the reader once he introduces

another character, Andrei's subversive brother Ivan Babichev. Nikolai meets him after glimpsing his reflection in a mirror on the street, the kind of literary trick practiced by Nabokov (though executed here with not quite the same dexterity). Nikolai quickly identifies Ivan as "my friend, teacher, and consoler"—his secret sharer. Ivan is an alternate Nikolai in antiquated costume, most notably a bowler hat. Like his brother Andrei, his apparent form isn't necessarily consistent with reality. If Andrei's character is defined by propagandistic bombast and Nikolai's malice, Ivan exists within rumors and hearsay: he's a poet, a dreamer, an inventor of a robot, and a rabble-rouser who breaks up weddings and stalks his brother at official functions. The rumors say that he's been interrogated by the GPU.

It's Nikolai's shiftlessness and his inability to adapt to the optimism of the new age that make him hate Andrei. Ivan is hardly more productive as a citizen, yet he's a malcontent with convictions, distinctly attached to a former way of life. He is said to tell the police that he leads an underground political movement whose goal is the preservation of "pity, tenderness, pride, jealousy, love—in short, nearly all the emotions comprised by the soul of the man in the era now coming to a close." The figmental organization appears to be less oppositional than conservational: people like his friend Nikolai must be saved because they are the repositories of classic human emotions. In Nikolai's case, the emotional essence is envy, the bane of the classless society.

The era's governing trope was the machine that would give rise to the envyless, emotionless, well-greased mechanized man, per the strictures laid down by the American efficiency expert Frederick Winslow Taylor (1856–1915), whose mathematical streamlining of the industrial workplace became integral to Marxist-Leninist practice. Given the communalization of personal life, exemplified by dining halls like the Two Bits, Taylorism was expected to regulate the most ordinary human relations and emotions. In Yevgeny Zamyatin's 1924 novel, *We*, men and women of the future shout at pro-government demonstrations "Long Live the Numbers!" and pursue "mathematical faultless happiness." His protagonist, D-503, believes that in the perfect Taylorist world, envy would be eradicated from the human psyche. *We* was too obvious a crack at the Bolshevik regime. It was banned in the Soviet Union, but a Russian-language edition was published abroad in 1927. The similarities in style and imagery suggest that *Envy* drew inspiration in part from a copy smuggled into Olesha's hands.

From the start, from that delightful rhapsody in the loo, *Envy* carries itself like a satirical novel, but the reader may find it hard to locate precisely the object of the satire. Even after we realize that Andrei is being maligned by the unreliable narrator, the satire still stings and the apparatchik comes off as buffoonish. Andrei's protégé, the young soccer player Volodya who's billed as a model "new man," seems no more than another dumb jock, with a mouth that's "a full, gleaming gearbox of teeth"—he's on his way to full mechanization, leaving behind his disgustingly human mentor. Yet Nikolai Kavalerov and Ivan Babichev are unappealing losers and neurotics, even more ridiculous than the apparatchik.

Despite these uncertainties, the novel was an immediate sensation in Russia, Olesha's fame spreading to Russian-language readers abroad (in Paris two years later, Nina Berberova wondered whether Nabokov would ever reach the stature of an "émigré Olesha"). The novel received praise from several leading Communist literary journals and, according to Andrew MacAndrew, a previous translator of Olesha's work, *Pravda* trumpeted that it exposed "the envy of small despicable people, the petty bourgeois flushed from their lairs by the revolution; those who are trying to initiate a 'conspiracy of feelings' against the majestic reorganization of our national economy and our daily life." The Party reading is perfectly sensible: the novel's five principal characters can be said to represent the Marxist-Leninist progression of history from romantic Ivan to the alienated intellectual Nikolai, the Party vanguard Andrei, the new proletarian Volodya, and, at the end of history, the beautiful, universally prized Valya, Ivan's daughter.

Olesha continued to win Party favor with his novel-length fable *Three Fat Men*, about a successful proletarian revolution in a storybook land; it was later filmed four times. Buoyed by his success, Olesha rewrote *Envy* as a play, *The Conspiracy of Feelings*, which was staged at Moscow's Vakhtangov Theater in 1929 and ran in repertory for two years. But by now the book was getting another look, raising questions. Was Andrei really the "positive hero" required by revolutionary culture? Didn't these avant-garde tricks emphasize literary form over ideological content? And doesn't *Envy* mysteriously side with Nikolai Kavalerov in his struggle against social progress?

No. Yes. Yes, especially. Nikolai is the mad, miserable true hero of *Envy*: the Underground Man, so close to our black hearts. Nikolai is wretched; so are we. Nikolai is debased; so are we. Nikolai is daily humiliated by the success of people who are more talented than he is, and also luckier, more energetic, more warmhearted, more forward-looking; so are we. The early readers' sympathy for Olesha's sad sack (and the resentment he directs toward a prominent Soviet official) indeed ran contrary to a regime that cast itself as a republic of heroes. Nikolai's recalcitrant, essentially human psychology would eventually doom the Soviet experiment and compromise other social engineering projects of the machine age, whoever owned the means of production.

In this respect, *Envy* reworked familiar contemporary themes. Virtually all Soviet writers of that time, confronted with a radically remapped world, were recording what the literary critic Marc Slonim called an "unending dialogue between man and the epoch." Virtually all searched for a definition of the new Soviet man. Doubts about this man's psychology could be tolerated, in 1927, without being labeled dissidence. Although not a Party member, Olesha considered himself a reliable fellow traveler, a *poputchik*. (He identified himself with Kavalerov, whose name suggests a cavalier, another kind of fellow traveler.) His absurdist spoof recalls *Dead Souls*, which lampooned universal human conceits while neither directly condemning serfdom nor envisioning an end to it.

The political criticism of *Envy* was insufficient to land Olesha in jail, but it appears to have cooled his career in the early 1930s. The novel and his short stories were allowed to go out of print and he found unobtrusive work in the cinema and as a critic, particularly for *Literaturnaya gazeta*. He joined Isaac Babel at the infamous 1934 First Congress of Soviet Writers, where they each half-defended their falloff in literary production, and half-apologized for it. In his speech, striking a plaintive note, Olesha confessed that he was uninspired by the themes demanded by socialist realism. While Babel was executed, Voronsky died in the camps, and Zamyatin was exiled, Olesha managed to survive the purges and the Great Patriotic War, spending some of those years making films and radio propaganda in Turkmenistan. After Stalin's death his books (including *Envy*) were reissued. He died in Moscow in 1960, suffering a heart attack as he proofread an article he had written about Ernest Hemingway. His nostalgic and apolitical unfinished memoir about the literary life, *No Day Without a Line*, was published in 1965.

The 1920s vision of a Taylorized world no longer provokes much foreboding. In ways that could not have been predicted even thirty years ago, computers and robotics are eliminating the most mechanically repetitive employment in the developed countries and seem destined to do so elsewhere. Yet other agents continue to work against the "conspiracy of feelings" that define us as individuals: globalized mass culture, consumerism, ever-sophisticated psychoactive drugs, religious fascism, and, in broadening swaths of territory around the world, more war. The electronic mass media fill our eyes and whisper in our ears, replacing reason with clichés and lies. *Envy* shows us Nikolai Kavalerov's world as he might have also seen our own: as false, overbearing, inhuman, and fractured.

—KEN KALFUS

ENVY

PART ONE

1

MORNINGS he sings on the toilet. You can imagine the joie de vivre, the health this man enjoys. The urge to sing bubbles up like a reflex. These songs of his, which have no melody or words, nothing but "ta-ra-ra," which he belts out in a variety of styles, go something like this:

"How sweet my life is ... ta-rá! ta-rá ... my bowels are flexing ... rá-ta-tá-ta-ra-rí ... the juices are flowing just right, straight through ... ra-tí-ta-doo-da-tá ... squeeze, bowels, squeeze ... tram-ba-ba-boom!"

In the morning, when he walks past me (I pretend to be sleeping) going from his room to the door that leads into the depths of the apartment, to the washroom, my imagination takes off after him. I hear the commotion there—it's a tight fit for his large body. His back rubs against the shut door, his elbows jut into the walls, he shifts from foot to foot. A matte oval glass has been set into the door. He flicks the switch, the oval lights up from inside, and it becomes a beautiful, opalescent egg. In my mind's eye I see that egg suspended in the hall's darkness.

He's carrying around six poods. Recently, walking down the stairs somewhere, he noticed his breasts bouncing in time to his steps. So he decided to add a new set of calisthenics.

This is an exemplary male specimen.

Usually he does his calisthenics not in his own bedroom but in the room with no specific purpose, the one where I'm staying. It's bigger and breezier, there's more light, more shine. Cool air pours in through the open balcony door. Not only that, there's a washstand here. The mat gets moved in from the bedroom. He's stripped to the waist, wearing knit drawers fastened by a single button in the middle of his belly. The room's blue-and-pink world revolves in the button's pearly lens. When he lies down on the mat on his back and starts lifting his legs in alternation, the button can't take it. His groin is exposed. His groin is magnificent. A tender scorch mark. A forbidden nook. The groin of a Producer. I saw a groin of the exact same sueded matteness once on a bitch antelope. One look from him and his girls, his secretaries and shopgirls, must get love shocks.

He washes up like a little boy: tootling, splashing, snorting, yipping. He grabs the water in fistfuls, and before he can get it to his armpits, he spills it on the mat. The water on the straw scatters in full, pure drops. Foam falls into the basin and bubbles up like a pancake. Sometimes the soap blinds him, and cursing, he wipes his eyelids with his thumbs. He squawks as he gargles. People stop under the balcony and crane their necks.

A very rosy, very quiet morning. Spring in full swing. Flower boxes on every windowsill. The vermilion of more flowering seeps through their cracks.

(Things don't like me. Furniture purposely sticks out its leg for me. A polished corner once literally bit me. My blanket and I have always had a complicated relationship. Soup served to me never cools. Any little thing—a coin or a cuff link—that falls off the table usually rolls away under furniture that's hard to move. I crawl across the floor and lifting my head I see the sideboard laughing.)

The dark blue straps of his suspenders hang down at his sides. He goes into the bedroom, finds his pince-nez on the chair, puts them on in front of the mirror, and returns to my room. Here, standing in the middle, he raises his suspender straps, both at once, as if hoisting a load onto his shoulders. He doesn't say a word to me. I pretend to be sleeping. The sun is concentrated in two burning bundles in the metal snaps of his suspenders. (Things like him.)

He doesn't need to comb his hair or put his beard and mustache aright. His head is cropped close, and his mustache is short—right up to his nose. He looks like a fat little boy all grown up.

He picks up the perfume bottle and the glass stopper chirps. He pours eau de cologne into his hand and passes his hand over the globe of his head—from forehead to nape and back.

In the morning he drinks two glasses of cold milk. He gets the pitcher out of the sideboard, pours, and drinks it all without sitting down.

My first impression of him knocked me out. I couldn't admit it or allow it. He was standing in front of me dressed in an elegant gray suit and smelling of eau de cologne. His lips were fresh and a little puffy. It turned out, he was a dandy.

Very often at night his snoring wakes me. Dazed, I can't figure out what's going on. It's as if someone were threatening me over and over again: "Krakatoa ... krra ... ka ... toaaa ..."

He was presented with this magnificent apartment. There's a vase standing by his balcony doors on a polished pedestal! A vase made of the finest porcelain, curved, tall, glowing red as if blood pulsed through it gently. It reminds me of a flamingo. An apartment on the fourth floor. The balcony hangs in a light-filled space. The broad suburban street looks like a highway. Across the way, down below, is a garden— the kind of garden that's typical of Moscow's outskirts, dense with ponderous trees, a chaotic assortment that has sprouted up inside the three walls of a vacant lot, as in an oven.

He's a glutton. He takes his meals elsewhere. Last night he came back hungry and decided to have a bite to eat. Nothing in the pantry. He went downstairs (the store on the corner) and brought back a real haul: two hundred fifty grams of ham, a can of sardines, pickled mackerel, a big long loaf, a good half-moon of Dutch cheese, four apples, ten eggs, and Persian Pea marmalade. He'd ordered an omelette and tea (the kitchen in the building is communal, it's manned by two cooks who take turns).

"Put on the feed bag, Kavalerov," he invited me, and fell to it himself. He ate the omelette straight from the skillet, chipping off pieces of egg white the way people chip enamel. His eyes grew bloodshot, he kept taking his pince-nez off and putting them back on, he smacked his lips, he snorted, and his ears wiggled.

I entertain myself with observations. Have you ever noticed that salt falls off the end of a knife without leaving a trace— the knife shines as if untouched; that pince-nez traverse the bridge of a nose like a bicycle; that man is surounded by tiny inscriptions, a sprawling anthill of tiny inscriptions: on forks, spoons, saucers, his pince-nez frames, his buttons, and his pencils? No one notices them. They're waging a battle for survival. They move in and out of view, even the huge sign letters! They rise up—class against class: the letters on the street plaques do battle with the letters on the posters.

He stuffed himself silly. He reached for an apple with his knife but only slit the apple's tawny peel before losing interest.

Once in a speech a people's commissar spoke of him with high praise: "Andrei Babichev is one of the state's most remarkable men."

He, Andrei Petrovich Babichev, is the director of the Food Industry Trust. He's a great sausage and pastry man and chef.

And I, Nikolai Kavalerov, am his jester.

2

He's in charge of everything that has to do with eating.

He's greedy and jealous. He'd like to cook all the omelettes, pies, and cutlets, bake all the bread himself. He'd like to give birth to food. He did give birth to the Two Bits.

He's raising his offspring well. Two Bits is going to be a giant of a building, the greatest cafeteria, the greatest kitchen. A two-course dinner's going to cost two bits.

War has been declared on kitchens.

You can consider a thousand kitchens vanquished.

He's putting an end to home cooking, eighths of pounds, and small bottles. He's assembling all the meat grinders, Primus stoves, skillets, faucets...Kitchen industrialization, you might call it.

He's set up several commissions. The vegetable-cleaning machines manufactured in the Soviet factory proved to be superb. A German engineer is building the kitchen. Babichev requisitions are being filled at all sorts of enterprises.

This is what I've learned about him:

One morning, he, the trust director, his briefcase under his arm—a very respectable citizen of obviously statesmanly mien—walked up an unfamiliar staircase amid the charms of the service entrance and knocked on the first door he came to. As Harun al-Rashid he was visiting one of the kitchens in a worker-inhabited apartment house on the outskirts of town. He saw soot and filth, crazed furies rushing about in the smoke, children crying. They fell upon him immediately. Huge, he was getting in everyone's way, taking up too much space, light, and air. Besides, he was carrying a briefcase and wearing pince-nez, all elegant and clean. And the furies decided that this had to be a member of some commission. Arms akimbo, the housewives tore into him. He left. Because of him (they shouted after him) the Primus stove had gone out, a glass was broken, and the soup was oversalted. He left without saying what he had meant to say. He has no imagination. He ought to have said this:

"Women! We're going to blow the soot off you, clean the smoke from your nostrils, the din from your ears, we're going to get you a potato that peels itself magically, in an instant, we're going to give you back the hours the kitchen has stolen from you—you're going to get half your life back. You, young wife, you cook your husband soup. You sacrifice half your day to a puddle of soup! We're going to transform your puddles into shimmering seas, we're going to ladle out cabbage soup by the ocean, pour kasha by the wheelbarrow, the blanc-mange is going to advance like a glacier! Listen, housewives, wait, this is what we're promising you: the tile floor bathed in sunlight, the copper kettles burnished, the saucers lily-white, the milk as heavy as quicksilver, and the smells rising from the soup so heavenly they'll be the envy of the flowers on your tables."

Like a fakir, he can be in ten places at one time.

He peppers his office memoranda with parentheses and underlining—he's afraid people won't understand and will mix something up.

Here are examples of his memoranda:

To Comrade Prokudin:
    Make candy wrappers (12 samples) that suit the buyer (chocolate, filling), but in the new way. Not "Rosa Lux-emburg" (I found out what that is—a pastille!!), though,

preferably something from science (something poetic
—"Geography"? "Astronomy"?), a serious name that
sounds enticing: "Eskimo"? "Telescope"? Report to me
by telephone tomorrow, Wednesday, between one and
two o'clock, at the office. Without fail.

To Comrade Fominsky:
  Tell them to put a piece of meat (neatly cut, like a
private butcher does) in each plate for the first course
(of both the 50- and 75-kopek dinners). Keep careful
track of this. Is it true that 1) they serve beer snacks
without trays? 2) the peas are small and poorly soaked?

He's petty, suspicious, and as fussy as an old housekeeper.

At ten o'clock in the morning he arrived from the cardboard
factory. Eight people were waiting to see him. He received 1)
the chief of smoking sheds, 2) the canning trust's Far Eastern
agent (he snatched a can of crab and ran out of the office to
show somebody, came back, set it down beside him, next to
his elbow, and for a long time could not calm down, constantly shooting looks at the blue can, laughing, scratching
his nose), 3) an engineer from the warehouse construction
site, 4) a German—regarding trucks (they spoke German; he
must have finished off the conversation with a proverb,
because it ended in rhyme and they both burst out laughing),
5) an artist who had brought the draft of an advertising poster
(he didn't like it—said it should be a muted blue—chemical,
not romantic), 6) some restaurant manager wearing studs
shaped like tiny milky-white bells, 7) a feeble little man with
a curly beard who talked about heads of cattle, and, finally, 8)
a delightful individual from the countryside. This last meeting was special. Babichev rose and moved forward, nearly

opening his arms wide. He filled the entire office—this capti-
vatingly clumsy, shy, smiling, sunburned, clear-eyed man,
this Levin straight out of Tolstoy. He smelled of wildflowers
and dairy dishes. They had a conversation about the state
farm. A dreamy expression came over the faces of all present.

At four twenty he left for a meeting with the Supreme
Economic Council.

3

In the evening, at home, he sits under a palm-green lamp-shade. In front of him are sheets of paper, notebooks, and scraps of paper with columns of numbers. He flips through the pages of his desk calendar, jumps up, searches the shelves, pulls out bundles, kneels on a chair, and—belly on desk, fat face propped on hands—reads. The desk's green expanse is covered with a sheet of glass. In the end, what's so special? A man working, a man at home, in the evening, working. A man staring at a sheet of paper and twisting a pencil in his ear. Nothing special. But his entire behavior says: You're a philistine, Kavalerov. Naturally, he doesn't say so. There's probably nothing of the kind in his thoughts, either. But it's tacitly implied. Some third party is telling me this. Some third party is making me rage as I observe him.

"Two bits! The Two Bits!" he cries. "The Two Bits!"

Suddenly he starts laughing. He has read something hilarious in his papers or seen something in the column of figures. He calls me over, choking with laughter. He neighs and pokes at the page. I look and see nothing. What did he find so funny? There, where I can't even distinguish the principles of comparison, he sees something so irregular that he's infected with laughter. I listen, horrified. It's the laughter of a heathen priest. I listen like a blind man listening to a rocket explode.

"You're a philistine, Kavalerov. You don't understand a thing."

He doesn't say this, but it's implied.

Sometimes he doesn't return until late at night. Then I receive instructions over the telephone.

"Is this Kavalerov? Listen, Kavalerov. I'm going to be getting a call from Bread and Bakeries. Have them call 2-73-05, extension 62, write it down. Did you write it down? Extension 62, the Main Concession Committee. Bye."

Bread and Bakeries is summoning Trust Director Babichev. Babichev's at the Main Concession Committee. What do I care? But I'm gratified because I'm taking an indirect part in the fate of Bread and Bakeries and Babichev. I experience administrative ecstasy. My role really is insignificant, though. A lackey's role. What's the matter? Do I respect him? Am I afraid of him? No. I don't think I'm any worse than he is. I'm no philistine. I'll prove it.

I feel like catching him out, exposing his vulnerabilities, finding a weak point. When I happened to see him for the first time at his morning toilette, I was sure I'd caught him, that his invulnerability had been breached.

Toweling off, he walked out of his room toward the balcony, and a meter and a half away from me, twisting the towel in his ears, he turned his back. I saw that back, that stout back, from behind, in the sunny light, and nearly cried out. The back gave everything away. The tender yellow of his fat body. The scroll of someone else's fate had unfolded before me. Old man Babichev had cared for his skin; the pads of fat had been softly distributed over his aging torso. My commissar inherited this thin skin, noble color, and pure pigmentation. And most important, what evoked real triumph in me, was the fact that on his waist I saw a mole, a special, inherited, aristocratic mole, the very same kind—blood-filled, a transparent, tender little thing that stood away from his body on a stem—by which mothers recognize stolen children decades later.

"You—a lord, Andrei Petrovich! Hah! You're a faker!" nearly tore from my lips.

But then he turned his chest toward me.

On his chest, under his right clavicle, there was a scar. It was round and a little rough, like the impression left by a coin on wax. As if a branch had grown on that spot and been chopped off. Babichev had done hard labor. He had attempted escape, and they had shot him.

"Who's Jocasta?" he asked me one day out of the blue. Unusual questions, unusual because of their abruptness, tend to leap from him (especially in the evenings). All day long he's busy. But his eyes slide over the advertisements and shop windows, and the tips of his ears catch words from other people's conversations. The raw material hits him. I'm his only unofficial interlocutor. He feels a need to start up a conversation, but he considers me incapable of serious conversation. He knows that people converse when they relax. He decides to pay some kind of homage to ordinary human wonts. He asks me idle questions. I answer. I'm an idiot around him. He thinks I'm an idiot.

"Do you like olives?" he asks.

"Yes, I know who Jocasta is! Yes, I like olives, but I don't want to answer idiotic questions. I don't think I'm stupider than you." That's how I should answer him. But I don't have the guts. He's crushing me.

4

I'VE BEEN living under his roof for two weeks. Two weeks ago he took me home, drunk, from the front door of the saloon...

I'd been thrown out of the saloon.

The fight at the saloon got going by degrees; at first nothing intimated scandal; on the contrary, a friendship might have started between the two tables. Drunks are sociable. The crowd where the woman was sitting suggested I join them, and I was all set to accept the invitation, but the woman, who was charming and skinny and was wearing a dark blue silk blouse that hung loose from her collarbone, made a crack about me, and I took offense and halfway there turned back to my own table, carrying my mug in front of me like a lantern.

That was when the jokes came raining down on me. And I really may have seemed ridiculous, like a shaggy piece of fruit. A man's hearty bass laugh pursued me. They lobbed peas at me. I walked around my table and sat down facing them; the beer sloshed onto the marble because I couldn't free my thumb, which was stuck in the mug handle. Tipsy, I broke out in confessions: abjection and arrogance flowed into a single bitter stream:

"You...troupe of monsters...an itinerant troupe of freaks who've kidnapped this young lady..." (The people around me listened up: the shaggy fruit was expressing himself oddly, his speech had risen above the general hubbub.) "You, sitting to the right under the little palm—you're freak number one. Get up and show yourself to everyone...Notice, comrades, most esteemed public...Quiet! Orchestra, a waltz! A neutral, melodious waltz! Your face looks like a harness. Your cheeks are nothing but wrinkles—reins, not wrinkles; your chin is an ox; your nose a coachman, like a bad case of leprosy, and the rest is a load of horseshit...Sit down. Next: monster number two...Are those cheeks or knees?...Very handsome! Admire it, citizens, a troupe of freaks is passing through...And what about you? How did you get through the door? Didn't you catch your ears? And you, glued to the kidnapped girl, ask her what she thinks about your blackheads. Comrades..." (I turned in every direction) "they...these ones here...they were laughing at me!? That one there was laughing...Do you know how you were laughing? You made the same sounds as an empty enema...Young lady... 'in gardens that the spring adorned, a tsaritsa came whom no rose could match, laying siege to all your eighteen years!...' Young lady! Scream! Call for help! We'll rescue you. What's happened to the world? He pinches you and you shiver? You like it?" (I paused and then said triumphantly) "Please, sit here with me. Why were you laughing at me? I stand before you, stranger girl, and I beg you: Don't lose me. Just stand up, push them aside, and step this way. What are you expecting from him, from all of them? What? Tenderness? Intelligence? Kindness? Devotion? Come to me. It's ridiculous for me even to compare myself to them. You'll get much more from me..."

I spoke, horrified at what I was saying. I recalled keenly those particular dreams when you know it's a dream, and you do what you want knowing you'll wake up. But here it was obvious that no waking was going to follow. The irrevocabilities were piling up at a furious pace.

I got thrown out.

I lay there unconscious. Later, when I woke up, I said, "I

invite them, but they don't come. I invite those pigs, and they don't come." (My words referred to all women collectively.)

I lay facedown on a grate in the sidewalk. There was something moldy under the grate. Something rustled in the black cube down there: the garbage was alive. Falling, for a moment I'd seen the grate, and the memory of it had governed my dream, which was a distillation of the alarm and terror I'd experienced at the saloon and the humiliation and dread of punishment, and in my dream it had turned into a chase scene—I was running away, trying to save myself, I'd marshaled all my strength, and then my dream broke off.

I opened my eyes, quivering with joy at my deliverance. But my waking was so incomplete that I perceived it as a transition from one vision to another, and in my new vision the leading role was played by my deliverer, he who had rescued me from the chase, that someone whose hands and sleeves I showered with kisses, thinking I was kissing in my sleep the one whose neck I had my arms around, weeping bitterly.

"Why am I so unlucky? ... Why is living in the world so hard for me!" I babbled.

"Stretch him out with his head up," said my savior.

I was being taken away in a car. Coming to, I saw the sky, the pale, too bright sky, racing from my heels and past my head. This vision thundered, it was dizzying, and each time it ended in a wave of nausea. When I woke up in the morning, in terror I reached for my legs. Before I'd even figured out where I was or what had happened to me, I remembered the jolts and the rocking. I was riveted by the thought that they'd taken me away in an ambulance, that they'd amputated this drunk's legs. And I reached out, confident that I was touching the thick, barrelish roundness of bandages. It turned out to be simple, though: I was lying on a sofa in a big, clean, light-filled room that had a balcony and two windows. It was early morning. The balcony's stone was warming up peacefully, turning pink.

When we introduced ourselves in the morning, I told him about myself.

"You looked pathetic," he said, "I felt so sorry for you. Are you insulted at someone meddling in a stranger's life, so to speak? If you are, then forgive me, please. But if you like, here's what. It would be fine for you to stay on. I'd be very glad to have you. There's lots of room. There's light and air. And there's a job for you: here—a little editing, selecting materials. How about it?"

What had compelled this famous individual to condescend to such a degree to a young, suspicious-looking stranger?

5

ONE EVENING, two secrets were revealed.

"Andrei Petrovich," I asked, "who is this, in the frame?"

On his desk stands a photograph of a swarthy young man.

"What's that?" He always asks me to repeat myself. His thoughts cling to his paper, he can't tear them away immediately. "What's that?" And he's gone again.

"Who is this young man?"

"Ah...That's Volodya Makarov. A remarkable young man." (He never speaks normally to me. It's as if I were incapable of asking him about anything serious. I always feel like I'm getting a proverb or a couplet from him in reply or—just mumbling. Now, instead of answering in an ordinary tone, "a remarkable young man," he declaims it, nearly goes into recitativo: "A re-maaark-a-ble young man!")

"What makes him so remarkable?" I asked, taking my revenge with the bitterness of my tone. But he didn't notice any bitterness.

"Oh, you know. Just a young man. A student. You're sleeping on his sofa," he said. "In point of fact, he's like a son to me. He's lived here for ten years. Volodya Makarov. He just went away. To see his father. In Murom."

"Ah, so that's how it is..."

"That's it."

He stood up from the desk and started to pace.

"He's eighteen. He's a famous soccer player."

("Ah, a soccer player," I thought.)

"Well now," I said, "that truly is remarkable! To be a famous soccer player—that truly is a great quality." (What am I saying?)

He didn't hear. He was in the grip of blissful thoughts. He was looking out from the balcony threshold into the distance, at the sky. He was thinking about Volodya Makarov.

"He is a youth absolutely unlike anyone else," he said all of a sudden, turning toward me. (I can see that the fact that I'm present, when this very same Volodya Makarov is in his thoughts, offends him.) "I owe him my life, first of all. He saved me from reprisals ten years ago. They were supposed to lay my nape on the anvil and strike me in the face with a hammer. He rescued me." (He likes talking about this deed. It's obvious he often recalls this deed.) "But that's not important. What's important is something else. He's a completely new man. Well, all right." (And he turned back to his desk.)

"Why did you pick me up and bring me here?"

"What's that? Huh?" he mumbled a second after he heard my question. "Why did I bring you here? You looked so pathetic. I couldn't help but take pity. You were sobbing. I felt so sorry for you."

"And the sofa?"

"What about the sofa?"

"But when your young man returns..."

Without thinking, he replied plainly and cheerfully, "Then you'll have to free up the sofa..."

I should have stood up and smashed his face in. You see, he'd taken pity, he, that celebrated individual, had pitied the unfortunate young man who'd lost his way. But only temporarily. Until his main guy returned. He just found the evenings dull. But later he'd drive me out. He was quite cynical about this.

"Andrei Petrovich," I said. "Do you realize what you just said? You're a lout!"

"What's that? Huh?" His thoughts broke away from his paper. Now his ear repeated my phrase to him, and I prayed fate that his ear was mistaken. Did he really hear? Well, let him. Once and for all.

But external circumstance intervened. I was not destined to fly out of this house just yet.

Outside, under the balcony, someone shouted, "Andrei!"

He turned his head.

"Andrei!"

He stood abruptly, pushing away from the table with the palm of his hand.

"Andryusha! My dear man!"

He walked onto the balcony. I went to the window. We both looked out. Darkness. The pavement was illuminated only here and there by windows. In the middle stood a squat little man.

"Good evening, Andryusha. How have you been? How's the Two Bits?"

(Through the window I could see the balcony and the hulking Andryusha. He was breathing hard, I could hear him.)

The man outside kept shouting, but somewhat softer.

"Why don't you say something? I came to tell you the news. I've invented a machine. The machine is called Ophelia."

Babichev quickly turned. His shadow fell sideways on the street and nearly stirred up a storm in the foliage of the garden across the way. He sat down at his desk. He drummed his fingers on its glass cover.

"Watch your back, Andrei!" the cry was heard. "Don't get too high and mighty! I'm going to bury you, Andrei..."

At that, Babichev jumped up again and with clenched fists flew out onto the balcony. The trees were definitely raging. His Buddha-like shadow came crashing down on the city.

"Who do you think you're fighting, you scoundrel?" he said. Then the railings shook. He struck his fist. "Who do you think you're fighting, you scoundrel? Get out of here. I'll have you arre-e-ested!"

"Goodbye," rang out from below. The tubby little man removed his hat, extended his arm, waved his hat (a bowler? I thought it was a bowler!); his manners were affected. Andrei was no longer on the balcony, and the little man, quickly scattering his little steps, retreated down the middle of the street.

"There!" Babichev shouted at me. "There, admire that. My dear brother, Ivan. What a swine!"

He was pacing, seething, around the room. And again he shouted at me.

"Who is he—Ivan? Who? A lazybones, a harmful, infectious man. He should be shot!"

(The swarthy young man in the portrait was smiling. He had a plebeian face. He flashed his gleaming teeth in a special, manly way. He exhibited a full glittering cage of teeth—like a Japanese.)

6

IT'S EVENING. He's working. I'm sitting on the sofa. Between us is a lamp. The lampshade (this is how I see it) obliterates the upper half of his face, it's gone. Hanging below the lampshade is the lower hemisphere of his head. Basically, it looks like a painted clay bank.

"My youth coincided with the youth of our era," I say.

He isn't listening. His indifference toward me is insulting.

"I often think about our era. Our era is renowned. Isn't it marvelous when the youth of an era and the youth of a man coincide?"

His ear picks up the rhythm. Rhythm is ridiculous to the serious.

"Of an era—of a man!" he repeats. (But go tell him he's just repeated some words he heard: he won't believe it.)

"Europe is wide open for someone talented to become famous. They like other people's fame there. Please, do something remarkable, and you'll be taken by the arm and led onto the road of fame . . . We don't have a path for individual success. That's true, isn't it?"

What happens is exactly what would happen if I'd been talking to myself. I make noises, utter words—oh, go ahead. My noisemaking doesn't bother him.

"In our country the paths to fame are strewn with barriers. A gifted person either has to fade away or else resolve to lift the barrier and make a great fuss. I, for example, feel like arguing. I feel like flexing my personality. I want fame of my own. Here we're afraid of paying attention to anyone. I want a lot of attention. I wish I'd been born in a small French town, grown up on dreams, set myself some lofty goal, and one fine day left my little town and walked to the capital and there, working fanatically, achieved my goal. But I wasn't born in the West. Now they tell me no one cares about anyone's individuality, the most remarkable individual is nothing. And gradually I'm adjusting to this truth, but it could be debated. I think, well, say you gain fame by becoming a musician, a writer, or a commander, or by crossing Niagara Falls on a rope . . . These are legitimate ways of gaining fame because the individual puts himself on the line . . . But, well, imagine when all people talk about is single-mindedness and utility, when what they want in you is a sober, realistic approach to things and events—it makes you want to jump up and hatch some obviously benighted plan, accomplish some brilliant piece of mischief and then say: 'Yes, you see you're like that and I'm like this.' Step out on the square, do something with yourself, and take your bow: 'I lived and I did what I wanted to.' "

He doesn't hear a thing.

"You might even go and kill yourself. Suicide for no good reason. To make trouble. To show that every person has the right to dispose of his own self. Even now. Hang yourself over the entryway.

"Even better, hang yourself over the entryway at the Council of People's Commissars, on Varvarskaya—it's Nogin now—Square. There's a great big arch there. Ever see it? That would be very effective."

In the room where I lived before I moved here there's a terrifying bed. I feared it like a ghost. It's as stiff as a barrel. It makes your bones rattle. I had a dark blue blanket on it that I'd bought in Kharkov, at the Blagoveshchensk fair, in a bad year. A woman was selling pies. They were covered with a blanket. Cooling, still not ready to give up the heat of life, they were virtually murmuring under the blanket, squirming like puppies. At the time I was living as badly as everyone else, and this picture breathed such well-being, hominess, and warmth that I made a firm decision that day to buy myself the very same kind of blanket. My dream came true. One fine evening I crawled under a dark blue blanket. I boiled under it and squirmed, the warmth made me jiggle as if I were made of gelatin. It was stupendous dropping off to sleep. But time passed, and the blanket's patterns swelled and turned into pretzels.

Now I sleep on an excellent sofa.

By intentionally stirring I make its taut new virginal springs twang. Separate, tripping rings emerge from its depths. I picture air bubbles streaming to the water's surface. I fall asleep like a baby. On the sofa I fly off into childhood. Bliss descends upon me. Like a child, I again know that brief interval of time between the initial drooping of eyelids, the first dropping off, and the beginning of real sleep. Once again I can draw out that interval, savor it, fill it with thoughts that suit me, and before I plunge into sleep, still exercising control over my waking consciousness, I can see my thoughts take on the flesh of dreams, transformed like bubbles rising from deep underwater to turn into fast rolling grapes, a hefty bunch of grapes, a whole fence full of thickly tangled bunches: a path alongside the grapes, a sunny road, heat...

I'm twenty-seven years old.

Changing my shirt once, I saw myself in the mirror and caught a striking likeness to my father. In reality, there is no such likeness. I recalled my parents' bedroom, and me, a small boy, watching my father change his shirt. I felt sorry for him. He couldn't be handsome and famous anymore, he was already set, finished, he couldn't be anything more than he already was. That's what I thought, pitying him and quietly taking pride in my own superiority. But now I've caught a glimpse of my father in myself. It's not a similarity of shapes —no, it's something else. I'd call it a generic similarity, as if I'd suddenly felt my father's seed in me, in my substantiation. As if someone had said to me: You're set. Finished. That's all there is. Sire a son.

I'm never going to be handsome or famous. I'm never going to come to the capital from a small town. I'm never going to be a commander, or a commissar, or a scholar, or a racer, or an adventurer. All my life I dreamed of an extraordinary love. Soon I'll be going back to my old apartment, to the room with the scary bed. The neighbors there are awful, especially the widow Prokopovich. She's forty-five, but in the courtyard they still call her Anichka. She cooks dinners for a collective of hairdressers. She set up a kitchen in the hallway. She has a hot plate in a badly lit niche. She feeds several kittens. Silent, scrawny kittens fly up after her hands with galvanic movements. She shakes out the giblets for them, so the floor looks like it's been decorated with pearly gobs of spit. Once I slipped on something's heart—small and tightly formed, like a chestnut. She goes around entangled in animal guts and sinew. A knife flashes in her hand. She tears through the guts with her elbows, like a princess tearing through a spider's web.

The widow Prokopovich is old, fat, and podgy. You could squeeze her out like liverwurst. In the morning I used to catch her at the washbasin in the hallway. She'd be half dressed and would give me a womanly smile. By her door, on a stool, was a basin, and in it floated the hair she had combed out.

The widow Prokopovich is the symbol of my male degradation. Here's how it works: Please, I'm ready, make a mistake with the doors at night, I'll leave it unlocked on purpose, I'll take you in. We can live and enjoy ourselves. But give up your dreams of extraordinary love. That's all past. Look at what you've become, neighbor: tubby, in trousers that are too short. Well, what else do you need? That one? With the slender arms? Your dream woman? With the pretty oval face? Forget it. You're a daddy now. Stretch out, okay? I've got a wonderful bed. My dearly departed won it in a lottery. A quilted coverlet. I'll look after you. I feel sorry for you. Okay?

Sometimes her look expressed frank indecency. Sometimes, when she ran into me, a small sound would come tumbling from her throat, a round vocal drop expelled by a spasm of delight.

"I'm no daddy, you hash-slinger! I'm no mate for you, you snake!"

I fall asleep on the Babichev sofa.

I dream that a lovely girl, laughing delicately, is crawling under the sheet with me. My dreams are coming true. But how, how do I thank her? I'm scared. No one has ever loved me for free. There've been prostitutes, but even they tried to get all they could out of me. What is she going to ask of me? As happens in dreams, she guesses my thoughts and says, "Oh, don't worry. Just two bits!"

I remember from years gone by: as a schoolboy, I was taken to the wax museum. In a glass cube a handsome man in a frock coat with a smoking wound in his chest was dying in someone's arms.

"This is French President Carnot, wounded by an anarchist," my father explained to me.

The president was dying, breathing, his eyelids were fluttering. The president's life was passing as slowly as a clock. I watched spellbound. A magnificent man lay there, his beard thrust forward, in a green-tinted cube. It was magnificent. Then for the first time I heard the rumble of time. Time was racing overhead. I swallowed ecstatic tears. I decided to become famous so that someday my wax double, replete with the rumbling of the ages, which only a few would be given to hear, would pose just like that in a green-tinted cube.

Now I write repertoire for showmen: monologues and couplets about tax inspectors, Soviet princesses, nepmen, and alimony.

> At the institute, what's all the clatter?
> What's all the fuss—what's the matter?
> Lizochka—the typist—Blum
> Is banging on her gift—a drum.

Still, maybe someday in the great panopticon there will be a wax figure of an odd, fat-nosed man with a pallid, good-natured face, disheveled hair, little-boy tubby, wearing a jacket with just one button left at the belly, and on the cube a small plaque: NIKOLAI KAVALEROV.

Nothing more. Just that. And everyone who sees it will say, "Ah!" And they'll be reminded of certain stories, legends maybe. "Ah! That's the one who lived in that famous time, who hated and envied everyone, who boasted, went overboard, let great plans get the better of him, who wanted to do so much and did nothing—and ended up committing a vile, repulsive crime . . ."

7

FROM TVERSKAYA I turned onto a side street. I needed to get
to Nikitskaya. It was early morning. The street was jointed. I
moved from joint to joint like a bad case of rheumatism.
Things don't like me. I'm hurting the street.

A tiny little man in a bowler was walking in front of me.

At first I thought he was in a hurry, but I soon discovered
that this way of a rushing along with his entire torso thrust
forward was altogether characteristic of the little man.

He was carrying a pillow. He was dangling a big pillow in a
yellowed slipcase behind his back. It kept hitting him on the
back of his knee, making dents come and go.

Sometimes, in the middle of town, in some side street,
they plant a romantic flowering hedge. We were walking
along beside a hedge of just that sort.

A bird on a branch flashed, jerked, and tapped, somehow
reminding me of hair clippers. The man walking ahead
turned to look at the bird. Walking behind, I caught a glimpse
of only the first phase, the half-moon of his face. He was
smiling.

"Truly, isn't there a similarity?" I nearly exclaimed, certain that the same similarity had occurred to him as well.

The bowler.

He removed it and wrapped one arm around it like an
Easter cake. His other hand held the pillow.

The windows were wide open. In one, on the third floor,
there was a dark blue bud vase with a flower. The little man
was drawn to the vase. He stepped off the sidewalk, walked

to the middle of the street, and stopped under the window, his face upturned. His bowler had slipped back on his head. He was holding the pillow tight. His knee was blooming feathers.

I observed from around the corner of a building.

He called out to the vase: "Valya!"

Immediately a girl in pink stormed to the window, upsetting the vase.

"Valya," he said, "I've come for you."

Silence fell. The water from the vase was running onto the ledge.

"Look what I brought...See?" He raised the pillow in front of his belly with both hands. "Recognize it? You used to sleep on it." He laughed. "Come back to me, Valya. Don't you want to? I'll show you Ophelia. Don't you want to?"

Silence again. The girl was resting facedown on the sill, hanging her tousled head. Next to her the vase was dripping. I remembered that a second after this girl's appearance, when she had hardly seen the man standing on the street, she'd already dropped her elbows to the sill, where her elbows had given way.

Clouds were crossing the sky and the windows, and their paths crossed in the windows.

"I beg you, Valya, come back. It's easy: run down the stairs."

He waited.

Gawkers were stopping.

"Don't you want to? Well then, goodbye."

He turned around, righted his bowler, and started down the middle of the street in my direction.

"Wait! Wait, Papa! Papa! Papa!"

He picked up speed and began to run. Past me. I saw he wasn't young. He was short of breath and pale from running. A silly-looking, tubby little man was running with a pillow pressed to his chest. But there was nothing crazy about it.

The window was empty.

She was running in pursuit. She ran as far as the corner—where the street's emptiness ended. She hadn't found him. I was standing by the hedge. The girl turned back. I walked toward her. She thought I might help, that I knew something, so she stopped. A tear swerved down her cheek like a drop on a vase. She was on tiptoe, preparing some passionate question, but I interrupted her, saying, "You whooshed by me like a branch full of leaves and flowers."

That evening I edit.

"...So the blood collected during the slaughter can be processed either for food, for sausage making, or for manufacturing clear or black albumen, glue, buttons, paints, fertilizers, and feed for livestock, poultry, and fish. The crude lard from all types of livestock and the fat-containing organic wastes are for the manufacture of edible fats, such as lard, margarine, artificial butter, and for technical lubricants, such as stearin, glycerin, and machine oil. Sheep heads and feet are processed, using electric drills, automatic cleaning machines, gas singers, chopping machines, and scalding vats, into foodstuffs, technical grease, cleaned hair, and bone for all types of goods..."

He's talking on the telephone. He gets ten or so calls an evening. Who knows whom he might be talking to? But suddenly this reaches me: "It is not cruelty."

I listen closer.

"It is not cruelty. You're asking me, and I'm telling you. This is not cruelty. No, no! You can rest perfectly easy. Do you hear me?...Humiliating himself? What? Walking around under windows?...Don't believe it. He's up to his little tricks. He walks around under my windows, too. He likes walking around under windows. I know him...What? Huh? Crying? All night? There's nothing to be crying all night about...Going crazy? Then it's off to Kanatchikov ...Ophelia? What Ophelia? Ah...Phooey. Ophelia—that's his raving... As you like. But I'm telling you, you're doing the wrong thing... Yes, yes... What? A pillow? Really?" A chuckle. "I can imagine... What's that? What's that? The one you used to sleep on? Imagine... What? What makes that pillow better than the one you're sleeping on now? Every pillow has a history of its own. In short, abandon all doubt ... What?... What's that?" At this he fell silent and listened for a long time. I was sitting on pins and needles. He burst into noisy laughter. "A branch? What? What kind of branch? Full of flowers?... Leaves and flowers? What?... Probably some alcoholic from his crew."

8

IMAGINE an ordinary tea sausage: a fat, perfectly round slice cut from the beginning of a hefty chunk. At its blind end, from the wrinkled casing tied in a knot, hangs a string tail. It's just sausage. Weight, probably a little more than a kilo. A sweating surface, yellowish dots of under-the-casing fat. Where it's cut, the same fat looks like white specks.

Babichev was holding the sausage in his hand. He was talking. Doors were opening. People were coming in. It was getting crowded. The sausage was resting in Babichev's raised pink hand like something alive.

"Great, isn't it?" he inquired, addressing everyone at once. "No, you have to look ... Too bad Shapiro's not here. We have to call Shapiro. Ho ho! Great! You called Shapiro? It's busy? Call again."

Then the sausage was on the table. Babichev lovingly arranged its bedding. Moving back and not taking his eye off it, he sat down in his armchair. He found it with his backside, dug his fists into the arms, and burst out laughing. He raised a fist, saw the grease on it, and licked it.

"Kavalerov!" (After the laughing.) "Are you free right now? Go to Shapiro, please. At the warehouse. You know it? Bring it straight to him." (With his eyes on the sausage.) "Bring it to him. Have him take a look and call me."

I took the sausage to Shapiro, at the warehouse. And Babichev kept trying to reach Shapiro.

"Yes, yes," he howled. "Yes! Absolutely superb! Let's send it to the exhibition. Let's send it to Milan! Yes, that one! Yes!

Yes! Seventy percent veal. A great victory...No, not half a ruble, you're crazy...Half a ruble! Ho ho! Thirty-five kopeks apiece. Great, isn't it? A beauty!"

He rode off.

His laughing face—a rosy jug—swayed in the window of the automobile. As he walked he handed the doorman his Tyrolean hat and, his eyes bugging out, ran up the stairs, heavy, noisy, and by fits and starts, like a wild boar. "The sausage!" was heard in many offices. "Yes, that one...I told you...What a story!" While I was still making my way through the sun-filled streets, he was calling Shapiro from each office: "He's bringing it to you! Solomon, you'll see! You'll burst...He still hasn't brought it? Ho ho, Solomon..."

He wiped his sweaty neck, reaching deep under his collar with his handkerchief, nearly tearing it, frowning, suffering.

I got to Shapiro's. Everyone saw me carrying the sausage, and everyone made way. A path was magically cleared. Everyone knew this was the messenger with the Babichev sausage. Shapiro, a melancholic old Jew with a nose that looked in profile like the number six, was standing in the warehouse yard under a wooden awning. The door, which was filled with the shifting summer darkness, like all doors that open out from storehouses (you see the same gently chaotic darkness if you shut your eyelids and squeeze), led into a huge shed. The telephone hung outside by the doorpost. Next to it, jutting out from the wall, was a nail with yellow pages of documents of some kind posted on it.

Shapiro took the log of sausage from me, tested it for weight, rolled it in his hand (rolling his head simultaneously), lifted it to his nose, and sniffed. After that, he ducked out from under the awning, put the sausage on a box, and with his penknife carefully cut a small, soft slice. In complete silence the slice was chewed, pressed to his palate, sucked, and slowly swallowed. His hand holding the penknife was held out to the side and it was trembling: the hand's owner was heeding his sensations.

"Ah," he sighed after swallowing. "Babichev is a wonder. He's made the sausage. Listen, it's true: he's done it. Thirty-five kopeks for that sausage—you know, it's really unbelievable."

The phone rang. Shapiro rose slowly and walked toward the door.

"Yes, Comrade Babichev. I congratulate you, I could kiss you."

There, wherever he was, Babichev was shouting so hard that here, a decent distance from the telephone, I could hear his voice, the crackling and popping in the receiver. The receiver, shaken by the powerful vibrations, nearly tore away from Shapiro's weak fingers. He actually shook his other hand at it, frowning, the way people wave at a naughty boy who is keeping them from hearing.

"What should I do?" I asked. "Will you keep the sausage?"

"He's asking you to bring it home to him, to the apartment. He's invited me to come eat it this evening."

I couldn't stand it.

"I'm actually supposed to bring it home? Couldn't he buy another?"

"You can't buy a sausage like this," Shapiro intoned. "It's not for sale yet. It's a test run from the factory."

"It's going to rot."

Shapiro, folding up his knife and sliding his hands down his side in search of his pocket, smiled faintly, his lids lowered, the way old Jews do. He spoke slowly, pedantically: "I congratulated Comrade Babichev on the sausage, which won't start stinking in just one day. Otherwise I wouldn't have congratulated Comrade Babichev. We're going to eat it up today. Put it in the sun, don't be afraid. In the hot sun it'll smell like a rose."

He vanished into the darkness of the shed, returned with paper, greased paper, and a few seconds later I was holding a masterfully assembled package.

From the very first days of my acquaintance with Babichev, I'd been hearing talk about the famous sausage. Somewhere experiments were being done to manufacture some special sort—nutritious, pure, and cheap. Babichev was constantly inquiring at one place or another; shifting to a concerned note, he would ask questions and give advice; sometimes gloomy, sometimes sweetly excited, he would walk away from the telephone. Finally the species was bred. Out of mysterious incubators crawled a fat, tightly stuffed casing, swinging heavily like an elephant's trunk.

When Babichev was given a piece of this stuffed gut, he turned bright red and was even embarrassed at first, like a bridegroom who has seen how splendid his young bride is and what an enchanting impression she's made on their guests. In happy distraction he looked at everyone and immediately put the piece down and pushed it away with a raised-palms expression that seemed to say: "No, no. No need. I'll just refuse. So I don't suffer after. Such successes can't happen in a simple human life. It's a trick of fate here. Take it away. I'm unworthy."

Carrying the kilo of marvelous sausage, I roamed in no particular direction.

I was standing on a bridge.

The Palace of Labor was on my left and behind me was the Kremlin. On the river were boats, swimmers. A cutter slipped quickly under my bird's-eye view. From this height, what I saw, instead of the cutter, looked like a gigantic almond cut lengthwise. The almond hid from view under the bridge. Only then did I recall the cutter's smokestack and the fact that near the smokestack two people were eating borscht from a kettle. A white puff of smoke, transparent and dissipating, flew in my direction. Before it could reach me, it shifted to other dimensions and touched me only with its final trace, twirling in a barely visible, astral hoop.

I was about to toss the sausage in the river.

A remarkable man, Andrei Babichev, a member of the society of political prisoners, a ruler, considered today a holiday. And all because they showed him a new type of sausage ... Did that really make it a holiday? Was this really glory?

He was beaming today. Yes, the mark of glory lay on him. Why wasn't I infatuated? Why wasn't I smiling and bowing at the sight of this glory? I was filled with spite. He, the ruler, the Communist, was building a new world. And in this new world, glory was sparked because a new kind of sausage had come from the sausage-maker's hands. I didn't understand this glory. What did it mean? Biographies, monuments, history had never told me of glory like this ... Did this mean the nature of glory had changed? Everywhere but here, in the world being built? Though I did feel that this new world being built was the chief, triumphant world. I wasn't blind. I had a head on my shoulders. No need to teach or explain to me. I was literate. It was in this world that I wanted glory! I wanted to beam the way Babichev was beaming today. But a new type of sausage was not going to make me beam.

I dashed through the streets with my bundle. A piece of lousy sausage was directing my movements, my will. I didn't want that!

A few times I was ready to chuck the bundle over a railing. But no sooner did I imagine the ill-fated piece of sausage freeing itself of its wrapper in flight, falling and disappearing torpedo-like in the waves, than another image instantly made me shudder. I saw Babichev advancing toward me, an ominous, insuperable idol with bugged-out eyes. I was afraid of him. He was crushing me. He didn't look at me—and he saw right through me. He didn't look at me. Only from the side could I see his eyes, and when his face was turned in my direction, there was no gaze, just the flashing pince-nez, two round, blind saucers. He wasn't interested in looking at me, he had neither the time nor the desire, but I realized that he saw right through me.

That evening Solomon Shapiro came, as did two others, and Babichev arranged the refreshments. The old Jew brought a bottle of vodka, and they drank, cutting bites of the famous sausage. I refused to participate in the feast. I watched them from the balcony.

Painting has immortalized many feasts. Commanders, doges, and plain old greasy gluttons have feasted. The eras have been engraved. Feathers wave, fabrics drape, cheeks quiver.

Today's Tiepolo! Hurry on over! Here are some feasting subjects for you... They're sitting under a bright, hundred-candle lamp, around a table, talking animatedly. Draw them, today's Tiepolo, draw *Feast at the Economic Planner's*!

I can imagine your canvas in a museum. I can see the visitors standing in front of your picture. They're perplexed, they don't know what's inspired the corpulent giant in the blue suspenders you've drawn... On his fork he's holding a slice of sausage. That slice should have vanished into the speaker's mouth long ago, but it can't because the speaker is too carried away with his speech. What is he talking about?

"We don't know how to make wurst!" the giant in the blue suspenders was saying. "Do you call what we have wurst? Quiet, Solomon. You're a Jew, you don't understand anything about wurst—you like that lean Kosher meat... We don't have wurst. Sclerotic fingers, not wurst. Real wurst should spurt. I'm going to do it, you wait and see, I'm going to make wurst like that."

9

WE WERE gathered at the airfield.

I say "we"! I was really just tagging along, for no good reason. No one spoke to me, no one took any interest in my impressions. I could have stayed home with a clear conscience.

A new model Soviet airplane was supposed to be making its maiden flight. They'd invited Babichev. The guests went behind the barrier. Babichev was the big cheese even in this select company. No sooner did he enter into conversation with someone than a circle formed around him. Everyone listened with respectful attention. He strutted in his gray suit—grandiose, head and shoulders above everyone else, and what an arch-span of shoulders it was! Black binoculars hung from a strap on his belly. When he listened to someone else talk, he would thrust his hands in his pockets and rock quietly from heel to toe and toe to heel on his widely planted legs. He scratched his nose a lot. After scratching he looked at his fingers, which he pinched together and brought close to his eyes. The listeners, like schoolchildren, involuntarily mimicked his movements and the play of his face. They scratched their noses, too, surprising themselves.

Enraged, I walked away from them. I was sitting in the snack bar drinking beer, caressed by a field breeze. I sipped my beer, watching the breeze fashion graceful ornaments out of my tablecloth's corners.

Many miracles had converged at the airfield: chamomile was blooming in the field here, very close by, near the barrier, ordinary chamomile blowing yellow pollen; there, down low, along the line of the horizon, round clouds rolled like puffs of cannon smoke; here, painted in the reddest lead, were wooden arrows pointing in various directions; there, high up, a silk tail—a wind sock—bobbed up and down, first dropping then blowing straight out; and there, across the grass, across the green grass of ancient battles, deer, and romance, crawled the flying machines. I savored this fancy, these delicious contrasts and combinations. The rhythm of the silk tail bobbing up and down disposed me to reflection.

Ever since I was a child, the name Lilienthal—transparent, quivering like insect wings—has sounded marvelous to me ...This name, which flew as if stretched over light bamboo planks, was linked in my memory with the dawn of aviation. Otto Lilienthal, an aviator, killed himself. Flying machines stopped looking like birds. Lightweight, transparently yellow wings were replaced by flippers. You could believe they beat the ground during takeoff. In any case, dust rises during takeoff. The flying machine now looks like a heavy fish. How quickly aviation became an industry!

A march thundered. The military commissar had arrived. Quickly, outstripping his companions, the military commissar walked down the lane. He created a wind with the pressure and speed of his pace. Leaves rushed after him. The orchestra played foppishly. The military commissar strode foppishly, too, quite to the orchestra's beat.

I rushed toward the fence, toward the gate onto the field. But they stopped me. A soldier said, "You can't go there," and put his hand on the gate's top bar.

"What do you mean?" I asked.

He turned around. His eyes were aimed at the interesting events unfolding. The designer and pilot, who was wearing a tan leather jacket, were standing in front, facing the military commissar. A tight strap crossed the military commissar's thickset back. Both were holding on to their visors. The motion had been sucked out of everything. Only the orchestra was in full swing. Babichev stood there with his belly jutting out.

"Let me through, Comrade!" I repeated, touching the soldier on the sleeve, and in reply I heard: "I'm going to remove you from the airfield."

"But I was there! I only went away for a minute. I'm with Babichev!"

I had to show an invitation. I didn't have one. Babichev had just taken me along. Of course, I didn't care if I got onto the field. Here, behind the barrier, was an excellent spot for observing. But I insisted. Something more important than the simple desire to see everything up close made me want to jump the fence. And it suddenly became very clear to me how much I didn't belong with these people who had been called together on this great and important occasion, the utter irrelevance of my presence among them, my irrelevance to everything great that these men had done—whether here in freedom or elsewhere, in other places.

"Comrade, I'm no ordinary citizen." I couldn't come up with a better phrase for sorting out the jumble that was my mind. "What am I to you? A philistine? Be so good as to let me through. I'm from there." I waved my hand at the group of people meeting the military commissar.

"You're not from there," the soldier smiled.

"Ask Comrade Babichev!"

I formed a mouthpiece with my hands and shouted. I rose on my tiptoes.

"Andrei Petrovich!"

Just then the orchestra stopped playing. The last beat of the drum trailed off with a subterranean rumble.

"Comrade Babichev!"

He heard. The military commissar turned around, too. Everyone turned around. The pilot raised his hand to his helmet, picturesquely warding off the sun.

I was terror-stricken. I was shifting from one foot to the

other here behind the barrier, a potbellied little man in trousers that were too short. How dare I distract them? And then silence ensued when they, still not sure who was calling one of them, froze in expectant poses—I found the strength inside me to call out one more time.

But he knew, he saw, he heard me calling him. One second—and it was all over. The group's participants resumed their former poses. I was ready to cry.

Then I rose up on tiptoe again, and through the same mouthpiece, drowning out the soldier, I sent a ringing howl to that inaccessible side: "Sausage-maker!"

And again: "Sausage-maker!"

And then several more times: "Sausage-maker! Sausage-maker! Sausage-maker!"

I saw only him, Babichev, in his Tyrolean hat, towering over the rest. I remember feeling like shutting my eyes and sitting down just outside the barrier. I don't remember whether I shut my eyes, but if I did, I still managed to see what was most important. Babichev's face turned toward me. For one tenth of a second it was turned toward me. It had no eyes. It had two blind, mercurially gleaming pince-nez disks. Fear of some immediate punishment sent me into a dreamlike state. I was dreaming. I was asleep, or so it seemed to me. And the most terrifying part of this dream was the fact that Babichev's head had turned toward me on a stationary torso, on its own axis, like on a screw. His back never turned.

10

I LEFT the airfield.

But the noisy celebration still drew me. I stopped on a green bank and stood, leaning against a tree, covered in dust. I was surrounded by a hedge, like a saint. I was breaking off the plant's tender, slightly sour twigs, sucking them and spitting them out. I was standing with my pale, good-natured face upturned, looking at the sky.

A machine took off from the airstrip. It soared overhead with a terrible purring, yellow in the sun, slanted like a dash, almost stripping the leaves off my tree. Higher, higher—I followed it, tramping along the bank of the stream: it was being carried off, first glinting, then black. The distance was changing, and it was taking on the shapes of various objects: a breechblock, a penknife, a trampled lilac blossom . . .

The triumph of the new Soviet machine's takeoff went ahead without me. War had been declared. I had insulted Babichev.

Now they were pouring out of the airfield gates in a throng. The drivers had already stepped lively. There was Babichev's blue car. Alpers, the driver, saw me and signaled. I turned my back on him. My shoes got caught in the green tangle of grass.

I had to talk to him. He had to understand. I had to explain to him that it was his fault, not mine. His fault! He wasn't alone when he came out. I had to talk to him eye to eye. He was going from there to the administration. I decided to head him off.

At the administration they said he was at the construction site now.

"The Two Bits? To the Two Bits then!"

The devil if I knew what to do; a certain word I needed to say to him had been on the tip of my tongue but had slipped away, and I was chasing it, racing, afraid I wouldn't catch up, afraid I'd lose it and forget it.

The construction site looked like a yellowish mirage hovering in the air. There it was, the Two Bits! Behind some apartment buildings, far away—individual wooded tracts merged into one mass that swarmed in the distance like the brightest of hives.

I was getting close. Clatter and dust. I'd gone deaf and had a cataract. I walked along the wooden planking. A sparrow flew down from a stump, the boards gave way a little, making me laugh about childhood memories of skating and overbalancing. I was walking, smiling at the way the shavings were settling and turning shoulders gray...

Where could I find him?

A truck was blocking my way. It just couldn't get in. It was bashing around, rearing up and nosing down, like a beetle climbing from a horizontal to a vertical plane.

The paths were confusing, I felt like I was walking through fish soup.

"Comrade Babichev?"

They pointed: that way. Somewhere they were knocking out barrel bottoms.

"Which way?"

"That way."

I was walking across a gully over an abyss. I was balancing. It looked like a ship's hold yawning below.

Immense, black, and cool. All in all, it reminded me of a wharf. I was in everyone's way.

"Which way?"

"That way."

He was slippery.

I caught a glimpse of him once: his torso was passing over some wooden planking. He disappeared. And then he reappeared above, far away—there was a huge void between us, everything that would soon be one of the building's courtyards.

He'd been delayed. Several men were still with him: peaked caps, aprons. I didn't care, I'd call out to him, to say one thing: Forgive me.

They pointed out the shortest route to the other side.

There was only a staircase left. Already I could hear voices. Just a few more steps...

But here's what happened. I had to bend over, otherwise he'd sweep me away. I bent over and grabbed the wooden step. He flew over me. Yes, he flew through the air.

At a wild angle I saw a figure flying yet stock-still—not a face, I only saw the nostrils: two holes, as if I were looking up at a monument.

What was that?

I rolled down the stairs.

He'd vanished. Flown away. Flown somewhere else on an iron wafer. A grated shadow accompanied his flight. He was standing on a piece of iron that described a semicircle with a clank and a howl. Not only that, there was a technical contraption, a crane. A platform made of girders, crisscrossed. Through the spaces, through the squares, I even saw his nostrils.

I sat down on a step.

"Where is he?" I asked.

The workers around me laughed, and I smiled in every direction, like a clown who's finished his opening number with a hilarious pratfall.

"It's not my fault," I said. "It's his."

11

I DECIDED not to go back.

My former quarters already belonged to someone else. A lock hung on the door. The new lodger was out. I remembered: the widow Prokopovich's face looked like a hanging lock. Was she really going to come back into my life?

My night was spent on the boulevard. The loveliest of mornings lavished itself overhead. A few other homeless men were sleeping nearby on benches. They lay, curled up, their hands slipped into their sleeves and pressed to their bellies, looking like Chinamen tied up and beheaded. Aurora tapped them with her cool fingers. They moaned and groaned, shook themselves, and sat up without opening their eyes or unfolding their arms.

The birds woke up. I heard little sounds: the little voices of the birds and the grass conversing. Pigeons had started to play in a brick niche.

Shivering, I got up. A yawn shook me like a dog.

(Gates were being opened. A glass was being filled with milk. Judges were issuing sentences. A man who had worked through the night walked to the window and was amazed, not recognizing the street in its unfamiliar lighting. A sick man asked to drink. A boy ran into the kitchen to see whether a mouse had been caught in the mousetrap. The morning had begun.)

That day I wrote Andrei Babichev a letter.

YURI OLESHA

I was at the Palace of Labor on Solyanka eating Nelson croquettes, drinking beer, and writing:

Dear Andrei Petrovich,

You took me in. You let me get close to you. I slept on your amazing sofa. You know how lousily I'd been living up till then. A blessed night fell. You pitied me and took in a drunk.

You wrapped me in linen sheets. The smoothness and coolness of the cloth seemed calculated to soothe my fevered state and ease my fears.

A blanket cover's bone buttons even came into my life, and in them—you just had to find the right spot— swam a ring of the rainbow. I recognized it right away. It had come back from a long-forgotten, very, very distant childhood corner of my memory.

I found *a place to lay my head*.

This very phrase was for me as poetic as the word *hoopla*.

You gave me *a place to lay my head*.

From the heights of well-being you brought down a cloud of a bed for me, a halo that clung to me with magical warmth, wrapping me in memories, bittersweet regrets, and hopes. I began hoping I'd regain much of what had been destined for my youth.

You did me a great favor, Andrei Petrovich!

Just think: a celebrated man took me in! A remarkable personage settled me in his own house. I want to express my feelings to you.

Actually, I have just one feeling: hatred.

I hate you, Comrade Babichev.

This letter is being written to take you down a peg.

From the very first days of my life with you I began knowing fear. You were crushing me. Sitting on me.

You're standing there in your drawers. The beery smell of sweat is spreading out. I look at you, and your face starts getting strangely bigger, your torso gets bigger—the clay of some sculpture, some idol, is blowing up, puffing out. I'm ready to scream.

Who gave him the right to crush me? What makes him better than me? Is he smarter? Richer of spirit? More delicately organized? Stronger? More important? Better not only by virtue of his position but by his essence, too? Why do I have to admit his superiority?

I asked myself these questions. Every day of observation gave me part of the answer. A month has gone by. I know the answer. And I'm not afraid of you anymore. You're just a stupid official. And nothing more. You weren't crushing me with the importance of your person. Oh no! Now I understand you perfectly, I can examine you, having put you in the palm of my hand. My fear of you has passed like a child's fancy. I've thrown you off. You're a phony.

At one time I was tortured by doubts. "Was I nothing compared to him?" I thought. "If I'm so ambitious, maybe he really is my example of a great man."

But it turned out you're just an official, ignorant and stupid, like all the officials who came before and will come after you. And like all officials, you're a petty tyrant. Only petty tyranny can explain the hurricane you raised over a piece of mediocre sausage, or the fact that you brought a young stranger in off the street. And maybe it was out of petty tyranny that you took in Volodya Makarov, about whom I know only that he's a soccer player. You're a lord. You need jesters and hangers-on. I'll bet this Volodya Makarov ran away from you because he couldn't bear the ridicule. You probably made a fool of him systematically, the same way you did of me.

You said that he lives with you like a son, that he saved your life, you even waxed poetic about him. I remember. But it's all a lie. You're embarrassed to admit your aristocratic tendencies. But I've seen the mole on your waist.

At first, when you said the sofa belonged to him and that, when he came back, I'd have to get the hell out, I was insulted. But a minute later I realized you were as cold and indifferent to him as you are to me. You're a lord and we're spongers.

But I'll be bold and assure you that neither he nor I— we're not coming back to you anymore. You don't respect people. He'll come back only if he's stupider than I am.

It's been my destiny that I have neither hard labor nor a revolutionary past behind me. They wouldn't assign me a job as important as manufacturing sparkling water or installing apiaries.

But does this mean I'm a bad son of my era and you're a good one? Does this mean I'm nothing and you're a big shot?

You found me on the street...

How stupidly you behaved!

On the street you decided: well, all right—he's a nonentity, let him work. An editor, by all means, a proofer, a reader, fine. You didn't condescend to a young man off the street. This showed just how smug you are. You're an official, Comrade Babichev.

What did you think I was? An endangered lumpen proletarian? Did you decide to support me? Thank you. I'm strong—do you hear that?—I'm strong enough to die and rise up and die again.

I wonder what you'll do when you read my letter. Maybe you'll try to get me deported, or maybe you'll put me in an insane asylum. You can do anything, you're a big man, a member of the government. You did say about your brother that he should be shot. You did say, "We'll lock him up at Kanatchikov."

I find your brother, who makes an unusual impression, enigmatic and incomprehensible. There's a secret here, but I have no idea what it is. The name "Ophelia" is strangely upsetting. I think you're afraid of it, too.

Nonetheless, I'm constructing some hypotheses. Some things I can predict. I'm going to stand in your way. Yes, I'm almost certain of that. Nonetheless, I won't let you. You want power over your brother's daughter. I've only seen her once. Yes, it was her I told you about with the branch full of leaves and flowers. You have no imagination. You laughed at me. I heard the telephone conversation. You blackened me in that girl's eyes the way you blackened him, her father. It doesn't pay for you to admit that a girl you want to conquer, to make your very own fool, the way you tried to make idiots out of us—you want that girl to have a gentle, lyrical soul. You want to exploit her, the way you exploit (I use this word of yours intentionally) "sheep heads and feet with the ingenious use of electric drills" (from your brochure).

But no, I won't let you. Why should I! Such a tasty morsel! You're a glutton. Would you really stop at anything for the sake of your physiology? What keeps you from seducing the girl? The fact that she's your niece? You laugh at family, at kin. You want to subdue her.

And that's the reason for your rabid ranting at your brother. Anyone else after barely glancing at him would say that this is a remarkable man. I think he's brilliant, and I don't even know him. Brilliant at what—I don't know... You're persecuting him. I heard you banging your fist on the railings. You made a daughter abandon her father.

But you aren't going to persecute me.

I'm going to stand up for your brother and his daughter. Listen, you blockhead, who laughed at a branch full of flowers and leaves, listen. Yes, that's the only way, only that exclamation could express my ecstasy at the sight of her. And what words do you prepare for her? You called me a drunk only because I addressed a young woman in figurative language you don't understand? I don't know whether it's laughable or scary. You're laughing now, but before long I'll have you scared to death. And don't think that's just a figure of speech—I can think very realistically, too. All right! I can talk about her, about Valya, using ordinary words, too. So here, if you'll allow me, I'll quote several definitions that you can understand, on purpose, to rile you, to taunt you with what you'll never get, esteemed sausage-maker.

Yes, she was standing in front of me—yes, first I'll tell you in my own way. She was lighter than a shadow. The lightest of shadows—the shadow of falling snow—might have envied her. Yes, first my way. She didn't listen to me with her ear, she listened with her temple, her head slightly tilted. Yes, her face is the color of a nut—from the sun—and the shape of a nut: her cheekbones, rounded, narrow to her chin. Can you understand that? No? Then here's more. Her dress was twisted from running, it had fallen open, and I saw that she wasn't tan all over, on her breast I saw the light blue curve of a vein...

And now—your way. The description of the one you want to feast on. Before me stood a young lady of about sixteen, still practically a girl, broad in the shoulders, gray-eyed, her hair cropped and tousled—an enchanting adolescent, slender as a chess piece (that's my way!), not very tall.

You won't get her.

She's going to be my wife. I've dreamed of her all my life.

Let's fight! Let's do battle! You're thirteen years older than me. Those years are behind you and ahead of me. One or two more achievements in the sausage business, one or two more cheap cafeterias—that's the limit of your career.

Oh, I dream of something else!

I'll get Valya, not you. We'll be a sensation in Europe, where they love fame.

I'll get Valya. She'll be my reward for everything: the humiliation, the youth I never had, my dog's life.

I've told you about the cook. Remember how she washes up in the hallway? Well, I'm going to see something else: a room somewhere. One day it'll be brightly lit by the sun, there'll be a dark blue washbasin by the window, and the window will dance in the basin, and Valya will be washing up at the basin, shimmering like a carp, splashing, tickling the ivories of the water . . .

I'll do everything to make sure this dream comes true. You aren't going to exploit Valya.

Goodbye, Comrade Babichev.

How could I have played such a demeaning role for a whole month? I'm never coming back to you. Wait. Maybe your first fool will come back. Give him my regards. What happiness that I won't have to go back to you anymore!

Every time my self-esteem suffers from anything, I know that immediately, by association, I'll remember one of the evenings spent near your desk. What upsetting visions!

It's evening. You're at your desk. You exude self-rapture. "I'm working"—these rays crackle. "Do you hear, Kavalerov? I'm working, don't bother me . . . tss . . . philistine."

And in the morning praise pours out of all different mouths: "A big man! An amazing man! A perfect individual—Andrei Petrovich Babichev!"

But you see, while the lickspittles were singing hymns to you, while smugness was puffing you up, a man was living by your side who nobody ever noticed or bothered to ask his opinion; a man was living there who followed your every movement, studying you, observing you, not from below, not servilely, but like a man, calmly, and he reached the conclusion that you're just a big-shot official—and that's all, a mediocre individual elevated to an enviable rank due to purely external circumstances.

It's no good playing the fool.

That's all I have to say.

You wanted to make me your jester, but I became your enemy. "Who are you fighting, you scoundrel?" you shouted at your brother. I don't know who you had in mind—yourself, your party, your factories, the stores, the apiaries—I don't know. But I'm fighting you: the most ordinary of aristocrats, an egoist, a voluptuary, a numskull confident that everything's going to work out for the best. I'm fighting for your brother, for the girl you've deceived, for the tenderness, the pathos, the individual, the names as disturbing as "Ophelia," everything that you're trying to crush, you remarkable man.

My regards to Solomon Shapiro.

12

THE CLEANING lady let me in. Babichev was gone. The customary glass of milk had been drunk and stood cloudy on the table. Next to it was a saucer and a cookie that looked like Hebrew letters.

Human life is insignificant. What's ominous is the movement of the spheres. When I settled here, a sun speck sat on the doorjamb at two in the afternoon. Thirty-six days passed. The speck jumped to the next room. The earth had completed another leg of its journey. The little sun speck, a child's plaything, reminds us of eternity.

I went out on the balcony.

On the street corner a cluster of people stood listening to the church bells ringing. The ringing was coming from a church I couldn't see from the balcony. This church was famous for its bell ringer. Idlers craned their necks. They could see the famous bell ringer at work.

Once I stood on the corner for a good hour. I could see inside the bell tower through the gaps in the arch. There, in the sooty darkness you find in attics, amid atticky beams wrapped in spiderwebs, the bell ringer was in a frenzy. Twenty bells were tearing him to pieces. Like a coachman, he was leaning back, dropping his head back, maybe even whooping. He was twisting at his waist, in the middle of a gloomy web of ropes, first pausing, then hanging from outstretched arms, then rushing into a corner, elbowing his way through the web's whole blueprint—an enigmatic musician, indistinguishable, dark, even ugly, like Quasimodo.

(Actually, the distance made him that frightening. If you like you could say: a little man wielding crockery and cymbals. You could call the ringing from the famous bell tower a combination of restaurant and train station clatter.)

I listened from the balcony.

"Tom-vir-lee-lee! Tom-vir-lee-lee! Tom-vir-lee-lee!"

Tom. Virleelee. Some Tom Virleelee was hovering in the air:

> Tom Virleelee,
> Tom with a knapsack,
> Young Tom Virleelee!

The disheveled bell-ringer transposed many of my mornings into music. *Tom* is the striking of the big bell, a big cauldron; *Virleelee* are the little cymbals.

Tom Virleelee pierced straight through me on one of the fine mornings I greeted under this roof. A musical phrase transformed into a verbal one. I had a vivid picture of this Tom.

A youth looking out over a city. A youth unknown to all draws near, sees the city, which is sleeping and suspects nothing. The morning fog is just now dispersing. The town swirls in the valley like a flickering gray cloud. Tom Virleelee, smiling and pressing his hand to his heart, looks down at the town, searching in its childish outlines for familiar scenes.

A knapsack on the youth's back.

He's going to do it all.

He's the youthful arrogance, the very secret spirit of proud dreams.

The days will pass, and soon (the sun speck won't have skipped from the doorjamb to the next room very many times) little boys, themselves dreaming of walking like that with a knapsack on their back through the outskirts of a town, the outskirts of fame, will sing a song about a man who did everything he wanted to do:

Tom Virleelee,
Tom with a knapsack,
Young Tom Virleelee!

Thus, the ringing of an ordinary Moscow church was transformed inside me, in my romantic, obviously Western European dream.

I was going to leave my letter on the desk, gather my belongings (in a knapsack?), and leave. The letter, folded into a square, I put on the glass cover, next to the portrait of someone I considered my comrade in misfortune.

Someone knocked at the door. Was it he?

I opened it.

In the doorway, holding a knapsack in his hand and smiling gaily (a Japanese smile), exactly as if he had seen through the door the dear friend cherished in his dreams, stood a shy young man who reminded me of Valya: Tom Virleelee.

This was the young troublemaker, Volodya Makarov. He looked at me in surprise, then quickly scanned the room. Several times his gaze returned to the sofa, down under the sofa, where my low boots peeped out.

"Hullo!" I greeted him.

He walked toward the sofa, sat down, paused a moment, then headed for the bedroom, spent some time in there, returned, and stopping next to the flamingo vase, asked me, "Where's Andrei Petrovich? At the office?"

"I can't swear to it. Andrei Petrovich will be back this evening. He may bring some new fool with him. You're the first, I'm the second, he'll be the third. Or were there other fools before you? Or maybe he'll bring the girl with him."

"Who?" asked Tom Virleelee. "What's that?" he asked, frowning in incomprehension. His temples tensed.

He sat back down on the sofa. My low boots under the sofa

bothered him. You could tell. He was not averse to touching them with the back of his boot.

"Why did you come back?" I asked. "Why the hell did you come back? Your role and mine are over. Now he's interested in someone else. He's debauching a girl. His niece, Valya. Get it? Get out of here. Listen to me!"

I rushed at him. He sat motionless.

"Listen to me! Do what I did! Tell him the whole truth . . . Here"—I snatched the letter from the desk—"here's the letter I wrote him . . ."

He held me at arm's length. His knapsack lay familiarly in the corner by the sofa. He walked over to the telephone and called the office.

My belongings stayed the way they were, uncollected.

I turned and ran.

13

I KEPT the letter. I'd decided to destroy it. The soccer player was living with him like a son. From the way his knapsack arranged itself in the corner, from the way he surveyed the room, picked up the telephone receiver, and called the number, you could tell he'd been there a long time, he was his own man here. This house was his. An ill-spent night had affected me. I hadn't written what I'd meant to write. Babichev wouldn't have understood my indignation. He would have written it off as envy. He would have thought I envied Volodya.

It's a good thing I kept the letter.

Otherwise I'd have fired a blank.

I was wrong in thinking that Volodya was his fool and entertainer. Consequently, in my letter I shouldn't have taken him under my wing. On the contrary. Now that I'd met him, I'd seen his arrogance. Babichev was harboring someone exactly like himself. He'd end up the same pompous, blind man.

His look said: Excuse me, you're wrong. You're the sponger. I have every right. I'm the rightful heir.

I was sitting on a bench. And here I discovered something terrible.

It turned out to be the wrong rectangle—mine was larger. This wasn't my letter. Mine was still there. In my haste I'd grabbed another. Here it was:

My dear Andrei Petrovich!

Greetings, greetings! Are you in good health? Aren't

you suffocating with your new lodger? Hasn't Ivan
Petrovich threatened you with Ophelia? Watch out:—
your Kavalerov and Ivan Petrovich—they're both going
to get drunk and do you in. Watch out, take care. You're
too softhearted, too easily hurt, so watch out . . .

Since when did you become so trusting? You let any
bum into your house. Tell him to get the hell out! The
very next day you could say, "Well, you've had a nice
rest, young man. Good-bye!" Just think: tenderness!
When I read your letter about how you'd been thinking
about me and that made you feel sorry for the drunk by
the wall, that you'd picked him up and brought him
home for my sake, because something bad might happen to me somewhere, as they say, and I might be lying
around like that. As soon as I read that I thought it was
funny and perplexing. It sounded like Ivan Petrovich,
not you.

So it was just as I'd thought. You took in this sly-
boots and then you lost your head, of course. You didn't
know what to do with him. And you felt funny asking
him to leave, so what were you to do? Who the hell
knows! Right? You see, I'm lecturing you. It's because
of the kind of work you do, it makes you oversensitive:
the fruits, herbs, bees, calves, all of that. Whereas I'm a
man of industry. You laugh, you laugh, Andrei Petrovich! You're always laughing at me. You see, I'm the
new generation.

What's going to happen now? Well, I'm coming back
—and what's going to happen with your eccentric?
What if your eccentric suddenly bursts into tears and
doesn't want to leave the sofa? You're going to feel
sorry for him. Yes, I'm jealous. I'll smash his ugly face
and drive him out. You're so nice—oh, you holler, bang
your fist, and swagger, but when it comes to taking
action—then you take pity. If not for me, Valya would

still be suffering with Ivan Petrovich! How are you keeping her there? She hasn't gone back, has she? You know yourself, Ivan Petrovich is a wily guy, he'll figure out how to insinuate himself, he's cheap goods, a charlatan. Right? So don't go feeling sorry for him.

Try this: put him in a clinic. He'll run away. Or suggest your Kavalerov go to the clinic! He'll be insulted.

Well, all right. Don't be angry. After all, your very words were: You teach me, Volodya, and I'll teach you. So here we are teaching each other.

I'll be back soon. In a few days. My papa sends his regards. Farewell, Murom-town! At night, when I'm walking, then I realize there isn't any town at all, actually, just factories. But the town—what's that? That's easy. It's what's left over after you take away the factories. Everything is for them, for their sake. The workshops above all. At night in the town the dark is positively Egyptian, gloomy, there are spirits here, you know. But on the outskirts, in the field, the factory lights burn and shine. It's a holiday!

But in town (I saw), a calf ran after a police inspector, after his briefcase (he was carrying it under his wing). Running, smacking its lips, chewing, oh well, the calf wanted it . . . This picture: a hedge, a puddle, the inspector is striding along in his red cap, fittingly, and the calf is aiming for his briefcase. Contradictions, you see.

I don't like those calves. I'm a man-machine. You won't recognize me. I've turned into a machine. If I haven't turned into one yet, I want to. Machines here are our beasts! Purebred! Remarkably indifferent, proud machines. Not like in your sausage factories. It's so primitive. You just cut up calves. I want to be a machine. I want to consult with you. I want to be proud of my work, proud because I work. In order to be indifferent, you see, toward everything that's not work! What

I envy is the machine. There's something! Why am I worse than the machine? We invented it, we created it, but it turned out to be much fiercer than we are. Give it its way, and it's off! It calculates so there's not a single extra figure. I want to be like that. You see, Andrei Petrovich—so that there's not a single extra figure. How I wish I could talk to you!

I imitate you to my utmost. I even chomp and chew like you do.

So many times I've thought about how lucky I've been! You lifted me up, Andrei Petrovich! Not all Komsomolers live like this. And I live with you, the wisest, most amazing individual. Anyone would pay dearly to live like that. You see, I know that lots of people envy me. Thank you, Andrei Petrovich. You mustn't laugh—I'm expressing my love, so to speak. A machine, you'll say, and he's expressing love. Right? No, I'm telling the truth: I'm going to be a machine.

How are things? Is the Two Bits under construction? Has anything caved in? How's Heat and Power? Did you get it set up? What about Kampfer?

And what's happening at home? Is the citizen-stranger still sleeping on my nice sofa? He's going to leave lice. Remember how they dragged me back from soccer? I can still feel it. Remember, they carried me in? And you got scared, Andrei Petrovich? You were scared, weren't you, Andrei Petrovich? You're my worrywart, you know. I'm lying on the sofa; my head feels as heavy as a train track. I'm watching you—you're at your desk, under the green lampshade, writing. I'm watching you—and suddenly you look at me and I shut my eyes right away, like with Mama!

About soccer, by the way. I'm going to be playing the Germans for the Moscow team. And maybe, if it's not Shukhov—on the USSR team. Beautiful!

How's Valya? Of course we're getting married! In four years. You laugh, you say we won't hold out. But I'm telling you here and now: in four years. Yes, I'm going to be the Edison of my era. The first time we kiss is going to be when you open your Two Bits. Yes. You don't believe it? She and I have a pact. You don't know anything. On the Two Bits opening day we're going to kiss on the podium to the music.

You'd better not forget me, Andrei Petrovich. I'm going to show up out of the blue and I'll find out that this Kavalerov is your best friend, I'm forgotten, and he's taken my place with you. He does calisthenics with you, goes to the construction site. What of it? But maybe he's turned out to be a remarkable fellow, much nicer than me. Maybe you and he have gotten to be friends, and I, the Edison of the new age, will have to get the hell out. Maybe you and he are sitting, with Ivan Petrovich and Valya, too, and laughing at me. Have your Kavalerov and Valya gotten married? Tell the truth. Then I'll kill you, Andrei Petrovich. Word of honor. For betraying our conversations, our plans. Get it?

Well, I'm all written out, I'm bothering a busy man. So there's not one extra figure—or I'll tell myself where to get off. This is because of being apart—right? Well, goodbye, my dear and much-esteemed man, goodbye. We'll be seeing each other soon.

14

A HUGE cloud with the outline of South America loomed over the city. The cloud itself was luminous, but the shadow it cast was ominous. The shadow was moving astronomically slowly toward Babichev's street.

Anyone who has ever stepped into the mouth of that street and gone against the current of people has seen the movement of the shadow, has started to black out. It's pulled the ground out from under their feet. It's like walking across a spinning sphere.

I've gone through it at their side.

The balcony hung in midair. On the railing lay a jacket. The ringing from the church had stopped. I took a loiterer's place on the corner. A young man appeared on the balcony. He was amazed how overcast it was. He lifted his head and looked out, leaning over the railing.

A staircase, a door. I knocked. My lapel was twitching from the pounding of my heart. I'd come to fight.

They let me in. Whoever opened the door stood back, pulling the door in. And the first thing I saw was Andrei Babichev. Andrei Babichev was standing in the middle of the room, his legs planted wide enough to let an army of Lilliputians pass between them. His hands were thrust into his trouser pockets. His jacket was unbuttoned and swept back. The hems on both sides, pushed back because his hands were in his pockets, looked like festoons. His stance said: What now?

He was all I saw. Volodya Makarov was all I heard.

I took a step toward Babichev. It was raining.

I was just about to fall to my knees in front of him. "Don't drive me away! Andrei Petrovich, don't drive me away! I've figured it all out. Believe in me like you believe in Volodya. Believe in me: I'm young, too, I'm going to be the Edison of the new era, too, I'm going to idolize you, too! How could I have missed it, how could I have been so blind not to do everything I could to make you like me! Forgive me, let me in, give me four years' time..."

But I didn't fall to my knees. I asked snidely, "Why aren't you at work?"

"Get the hell out of here!" I heard in reply.

He replied instantly, as if it had all been prearranged between us. But his reply reached my consciousness after a brief delay.

Something extraordinary happened.

It was raining. Maybe there was lightning.

I don't want to speak figuratively. I want to speak plainly. I once read *The Atmosphere* by Camille Flammarion. (What a planetary name! Flammarion—it's a star itself!) He describes spherical lightning and its amazing effect: a full, smooth sphere silently rolls around a building, filling it with blinding light... Oh, I haven't the least intention of resorting to banal comparisons. But the cloud was suspicious. Its shadow was advancing like in a dream. It was raining. A window was open in the bedroom. You shouldn't leave windows open in a storm! The draft!

In the rain, with its drops bitter as tears, through the gusts of wind under which the flamingo vase ran like a flame, igniting the curtains, which were also rippling under the ceiling, Valya emerged from the bedroom.

I was stunned to see her, but there was a simple explanation: a friend had arrived, his friends had rushed over to see him.

Babichev may have stopped by for Valya, who may have been dreaming of this day. It's all very simple. And I should be sent to a clinic, for treatment by hypnosis, so that I stop thinking in images, so that I stop ascribing to the young woman the effects of spherical lightning.

I am going to spoil the simplicity for you!

"Get the hell out of here!" my ear repeated.

"It's not quite that simple..." I began.

There was a draft. The door was still open. The wind sprouted on me like a single wing. It beat madly over my shoulder, blowing on my eyelids. The draft anesthetized half my face.

"It's not quite that simple," I said, pressing up against the doorjamb to try to snap off the horrible wing. "You went away, Volodya, and in that time Babichev was living with Valya. While you're waiting four years, Andrei Petrovich was going to spoil Valya so much..."

I wound up on the other side of the door. Half my face was anesthetized. Maybe I hadn't felt the punch.

The lock clicked, just like a branch breaking overhead, and I dropped from the beautiful tree with a thud, an overripe, lazy fruit.

"It's all over," I said calmly, getting up. "Now I'm going to kill you, Comrade Babichev."

15

I⊤ WAS raining.

The rain was heading down Tsvetnaya, hanging about the circus, turning onto the boulevards, to the right, and when it reached the Petrovsky Heights, suddenly it went blind and lost confidence.

I crossed the "Pipe," thinking about the fantastic fencer who walked in the rain, spearing drops with his rapier. The rapier glinted, the hems of his tunic fluttered, the fencer twisted, drops scattered, like a flute—and it was dry. He had inherited his father's legacy. I was soaked through to the ribs, and I seemed to have received a slap in the face.

I find that a landscape observed through the wrong end of binoculars is more lustrous and brilliant, more stereoscopic. Colors and contours sharpen up somehow. A thing, while remaining familiar, suddenly proves ridiculously small and unfamiliar. This gives the observer childish ideas. It's like a dream. Notice, someone who turns his binoculars around starts smiling incandescently.

After the rain the city became lustrous and stereoscopic. Everyone saw it: the trolley, colored carmine; the cobblestones far from monochromatic, among them even green ones; a housepainter high above emerged from the niche where he'd taken shelter from the rain, like a pigeon, and started in on his canvas of bricks; a boy in a window caught the sun in a shard of mirror...

I bought an egg and a French roll from an old lady. I

knocked the egg on the trolley post right in front of the passengers flying from the Petrovsky Gates.

I started uphill. The benches went by at knee height. At this point the lane bulged a little. Resplendent mothers were sitting on the benches, having spread out kerchiefs first. Their eyes—the color of fish scales—shone in their suntanned faces. A tan covered their necks and shoulders as well. But their large young breasts, visible in their blouses, were white. Lonely and banished, I sadly drank in this whiteness, whose name was milk, motherhood, matrimony, pride, and purity.

A nanny held an infant dressed up like the Pope.

A seed hung from the lip of a little girl in a red headband. The little girl was listening to the orchestra, not noticing she had crawled into a puddle. The tubas looked like elephant ears.

To everyone—the mothers, nannies, little girls, and musicians tangled up in their horns—I was a funnyman. The trumpeters cast sidelong glances at me, puffing their cheeks out even more. The little girl giggled because the seed had finally dropped. At this she also discovered the puddle. She blamed me for her failure and turned away in spite.

I'll prove I'm no funnyman. No one understands me. The incomprehensible seems either funny or scary. Now everyone's going to be scared.

I walked over to a street mirror.

I'm very fond of street mirrors. They pop up along your path. Your path is ordinary, calm—the usual city path, promising neither miracles nor visions. You're walking along, not assuming anything, you raise your eyes, and suddenly, for a moment, it's all clear to you: the world and its rules have undergone unprecedented changes.

Optics and geometry—the essence of what had been your motion, your movement, your desire to go exactly where you were going—have been laid waste. You start thinking you

have eyes in back of your head; you even smile distractedly at passersby, you're embarrassed by this advantage of yours.

"Ah," you sigh quietly.

The trolley, which had just gone out of sight, again rushes in front of you, cutting across the edge of the boulevard like a knife through cake. A straw hat hanging on a blue ribbon over someone's arm (just this minute you saw her, she caught your attention, but you didn't think to look around), comes back now, floating past your eyes.

A vista opens up before you. You're sure this is a building, a wall, but you have an advantage: it's not a building! You've discovered a secret. There is no wall. Here you have a mysterious world where everything you've just seen is repeated—and repeated with that vivid stereoscopic quality that is in the exclusive power of the binoculars' wrong end.

You don't know which way is up, as the saying goes. So suddenly have the rules been broken, so incredibly have the proportions changed. But you rejoice in your dizziness... Having guessed, you rush toward the blue square. Your face is suspended, motionless in the mirror, it alone has natural forms, it alone is a particle left over from the regular world, while everything else has collapsed, changed, and taken on a new regularity that you just can't master, even after standing a whole hour in front of the mirror, where your face looks like it's in a tropical garden. The vegetation is too green, the sky too blue.

You just can't say for certain (until you turn away from the mirror) which direction a pedestrian you've observed in the mirror is headed... If you just turned around...

I watched myself in the mirror finishing my roll.

I turned around.

Someone was walking toward the mirror, having appeared from the side. I blocked his reflection. The smile he had prepared for himself came to me instead. He was a head shorter than me and looked up.

He rushed toward the mirror to find and flick off the caterpillar that had landed on the far end of his shoulder. And he did flick it off, twisting his shoulder forward like a fiddler.

I continued to think about optical illusions and mirror tricks and so asked this man before I recognized him: "Which direction did you come from? Where did you come from?"

"Where?" he repeated. "Where did I come from?" He looked at me with clear eyes. "I dreamed myself up."

He took off his bowler, revealing a bald spot, and bowed with exaggerated stylishness. The way a has-been greets his benefactor. And like a has-been, he had bags under his eyes that sagged like purple stockings. He was sucking on a candy.

I immediately recognized my friend, teacher, and consoler.

I grabbed his hand, and nearly prostrating myself before him, began: "Tell me, answer me."

He lifted his eyebrows.

"What is this . . . Ophelia?"

He was about to answer. But a drool of fruit-drop leaked through a corner of his lips like sweet juice. Thrilled and moved, I awaited his reply.

PART TWO

1

THE APPROACH of old age did not scare Ivan Babichev.

Sometimes complaints did actually come from his lips over his quickly passing life, his lost years, his presumed stomach cancer...But these complaints were too sunny—probably even flat-out insincere. Complaints of a rhetorical nature.

Sometimes, placing his hand on the left side of his chest, he would smile and ask, "I wonder what sound a breaking heart makes?"

Once he raised his arm to show his friends the back of his hand, where the veins were laid out in the shape of a tree, and he broke out in the following improvisation:

"Here," he said, "is the tree of life. Here is a tree that tells me more about life and death than the flowering and fading trees of gardens. I don't remember when exactly I discovered that my wrist was blooming like a tree...but it must have been during that wonderful time when the flowering and fading of trees still spoke to me not of life and death but of the end and beginning of the school year! It was blue then, this tree, blue and slender, and the blood, which at the time I thought of not as a liquid but as light, rose like the dawn over it and turned my metacarpus's entire landscape into a Japanese watercolor...

"The years passed, I changed, and the tree changed, too.

"I remember a splendid time; the tree was spreading. The pride I felt, seeing its inexorable flowering! It became gnarled and reddish brown—and therein lay its strength! I could call it my hand's mighty rigging. But now, my friends! How decrepit it is, how rotten!

"The branches seem to be breaking off, cavities have appeared...It's sclerosis, my friends! And the fact that the skin is getting glassy, and the tissue beneath it is squishy—isn't this a fog settling on the tree of my life, the fog that will soon envelop all of me?"

There had been three Babichev brothers. Ivan was the second. The oldest was called Roman. He had been a member of a militant organization and had been executed for his part in a terrorist act.

The youngest brother, Andrei, had emigrated. "How do you like that, Andrei?" Ivan wrote to him in Paris. "We have a martyr in the family! If only that would make Granny happy!" To which brother Andrei, with his characteristic rudeness, curtly replied, "You're nothing but a scoundrel." Thus was the disagreement between the brothers defined.

Ever since childhood, Ivan had amazed his family and friends.

As a twelve-year-old boy, he had demonstrated inside the family circle a strange type of instrument, sort of like a lampshade with a fringe of little bells, and assured them that he could use his instrument to summon up—on order—any dream for anyone.

"Fine," said his father, a school principal and a Latinist. "I believe you. I want a dream out of Roman history." ("What exactly?" the boy asked pragmatically.) "I don't care. The battle at Pharsalus. But if it doesn't work, I'm going to tan your hide."

Late that night a wonderful ringing receded, flitted from room to room. The school principal was lying in his study, even and straight, out of pure spite, like in a coffin. Ivan's mother was hovering by the peevishly closed doors. Little Vanya, smiling good-naturedly, was passing next to the sofa, shaking his lampshade, the way a tightrope walker shakes his

Chinese umbrella. In the morning, in three bounds, before he was dressed, his father raced from his study to the nursery and dragged fat, good, sleepy, lazy Vanya out of bed. The day was still tentative, something may have come of it yet, but the principal tore open the curtains, falsely welcoming the coming of morning. His mother wanted to stop the beating, his mother put her hands together, exclaiming, "Don't beat him, Petenka, don't beat him...He made a mistake...I give you my word...What, you mean you didn't dream it?...The ringing was going in the other direction. You know what kind of apartment we have...damp. I saw the battle at Pharsalus, I did! I dreamed the battle, Petenka!"

"Don't lie," said the principal. "Tell me the details. How were the uniforms of the Balearic archers different from the uniforms of the Numidian slingers?...Wellllll?"

He waited a moment, Vanya's mother was sobbing, and the little experimenter got a beating. He conducted himself as if he were Galileo. That same evening, the maid told her mistress that she was not going to accept the proposal of a certain Dobrodeyev. "He's always lying, you can't believe him," the maid explained it. "All night I dreamed of horses. They were all galloping, all terrible horses, like they were wearing masks. And seeing a horse means a lie."

The mother's jaw wouldn't stop trembling. She ran—like a lunatic—to the doors of the study. The cook was struck dumb at the oven; her jaw wouldn't stop trembling either.

The wife touched her husband's shoulder. He was sitting at his desk, reattaching his monogram to his cigar box.

And the mother babbled, "Petrusha, ask Frosya...I think Frosya dreamed the battle at Pharsalus..."

No one knows what the principal thought of the maid's dream. As for Ivan, we know that a month or two after the story with the artificial dreams, he was already talking about his new invention.

Apparently he had invented a special liquid soap and a

special pipe, which produced an amazing soap bubble. This soap bubble would get bigger as it flew, reaching first the size of a Christmas tree ornament, then a toy ball, then a globe as wide as a dacha flowerbed, and on and on all the way to the size of a barrage balloon—and then it would burst, showering the city with a brief golden shower.

His father was in the kitchen. (He was one of that gloomy clan of fathers who takes pride in his knowledge of certain culinary secrets and who considers it his exclusive privilege, say, to determine the number of bay leaves necessary for some famed soup that had been handed down from generation to generation, or, say, to observe how long eggs should remain in the pot in order to achieve the ideal "coddled" state.)

Outside the kitchen window, in the small courtyard, against the wall, little Ivan was spinning tales. His father, who was listening with his yellow ear, looked out. Little boys had gathered around Ivan. And Ivan was lying about the soap bubble. It was going to be as big as a hot-air balloon.

Once again bile bubbled up inside the principal. The year before, his oldest son Roman had left the family. The father had taken it out on his younger sons.

God had used his sons to offend him.

He retreated from the window, actually smiling out of malice. At dinner he waited for Ivan's pronouncements, but Ivan didn't make a peep. "I see he despises me. I see he thinks I'm a fool," the principal seethed. And at the end of the day, when father Babichev was drinking tea on the balcony, suddenly somewhere very far away, in the very back background, which was melting, glassy, flittering fine and yellow in the rays of the setting sun, a large orange globe appeared in his field of vision. It was sailing slowly, crossing the field on a slant...

The principal poked his head inside, and through a crack in the door saw Ivan just then on the windowsill in the next room. The schoolboy, looking hard out the window, was clapping his hands loudly.

"I achieved great satisfaction that day," recalled Ivan Petrovich. "My father was frightened. For a long time after that I tried to meet his eyes, but he averted them. And I began to feel sorry for him. His face turned gray. I thought he was going to die. And I magnanimously cast off the mantle. He was a dry man, my papa, petty but inattentive. He didn't know that on that day the aeronaut Ernest Vitollo was flying over the city. Marvelous posters had announced this. I confessed to cheating unwittingly. I must tell you that my soap-bubble experiments did not lead to my longed-for results."

(The facts attest that when Ivan Babichev was a twelve-year-old schoolboy, ballooning had not yet reached widespread development, and it's unlikely that flights would have been arranged in those days over a provincial town.

But what if he had made this up? Who cares! Making things up is what reason likes best.)

His friends delighted in Ivan Babichev's improvisations.

"And it seems to me that the night after that grievous day, my papa dreamed of the battle at Pharsalus. He didn't go to school in the morning. Mama brought him his mineral water in the study. The details of the battle must have shaken him. Maybe he couldn't reconcile himself to this mockery of history which his dream had indulged in... He may have dreamed that the battle's outcome was decided by Balearic archers flying in on hot-air balloons..."

With this ending Ivan Babichev concluded his tale of soap bubbles.

The next time he shared with his friends the following incident from his adolescence:

"A student, by the last name of Shemiot, was courting a young lady, but you know I don't remember the young lady's name... let's... let's... let's say the name of the young lady who stamped her heels like a goat was Lilya Kapitanaki. All the boys knew what was going on in her yard. The student would stand sentry under Lilya's balcony, all set but afraid to summon from the golden depths of the balcony door this girl who was probably sixteen and who seemed to us boys like an old lady.

"The student's cap was blue, his cheeks red. The student rode up on his bicycle. Indescribable was the student's melancholy when one Sunday, in May, one of those Sundays that number no more than ten in the memory of meteorological science, one Sunday when the breeze was so sweet and kind you felt like tying a blue ribbon to it, the student, having swooped up to the balcony, saw Lilya's auntie leaning on the railing, as gaudy and florid as the slipcover in a small-town guesthouse—all curls, spirals, and twists, and with her hair done up like a snail... And the auntie was obviously over-joyed at the appearance of student Shemiot; from high up she opened her arms, you might say, to the student and pro-claimed in a potato voice, the kind of voice that's wet with saliva and full of tongue, she said, exactly as if she were eat-ing a casserole: 'But Lilya's leaving for Kherson. She's leaving today. At seven forty. She's going away for a long time. She's going away for the whole summer. She told me to send her greetings, Sergei Sergeyevich! Greetings!'

"But the student, with the instinct of a lover, understood all. He knew that Lilya was sobbing in the golden depths of her room, that she was dying to go to the balcony and see, without being seen, the student, whose white, high-collared jacket absorbed, following the laws of physics, the greatest number of rays and shone with a blinding Alpine whiteness; but she couldn't go out because her aunt was all-powerful...

"'Give me your bicycle, and I'll avenge you,' I told the stu-dent. 'I know Lilya didn't want to go anywhere. There's been a tremendous ruckus and they're sending her packing. Give me your bicycle.'

"'How are you going to avenge me?' the student asked,

scared of me. And a few days later, with an innocent look, I brought Lilya's aunt some wart ointment, saying it was from my mama. By her lower lip, in the cleft, the aunt had a giant wart. This aging lady kissed me, and not only that but her kisses made me feel exactly as if I'd been shot point-blank with a new slingshot ... My friends, the student was avenged. Out of the aunt's wart grew a flower, a modest bluebell. It trembled delicately whenever the aunt exhaled. She was disgraced. With arms raised to the heavens, the aunt rushed around the yard, sending everyone into a panic ...

"My joy was twofold. First of all, my experiment at growing flowers from warts had succeeded brilliantly, and secondly, the student had given me his bicycle. And in that day, my friends, a bicycle was a rarity. At that time, they were still drawing cartoons of bicyclists."

"But what happened to the aunt?"

"Oh, my friend! She lived with the flower until the autumn. She waited in hopes of windy days, and when the day finally came, she set out by the back roads, skirting the livelier parts of town, for somewhere green ... She was wracked by moral agonies. She hid her face in her scarf, the flower lovingly tickled her lips, and this tickling sounded like the whisper of her misspent youth, like the specter of a lone, nearly trampled kiss ... She stopped on a hilltop and lowered her scarf.

"'Take it away, then, take it to the four corners of the earth! Blow, then, blow off its accursed petals,' she prayed.

"The wind died down, as if out of spite. But then a mad bee flew up from a nearby dacha, aimed for the flower, and began making buzzing figure eights around the poor woman. The aunt took flight, and at home, ordering the servant not to let anyone in, sat in front of the mirror, looking at her mythic, flower-adorned face, which swelled up before her very eyes from the sting so that it looked like some tropical root. Horrors! But simply to cut the flower off—that would be too risky. It was a wart after all! What if the blood suddenly were infected!

"Vanya Babichev was a jack of all trades. He composed verse and musical skits, drew excellently, knew how to do so many things—he even made up a dance intended to take advantage of his own physical characteristics: his plumpness and indolence. He was a clod (like many remarkable men in their adolescence). The dance was called the Jug. He sold kites, whistles, and Chinese lanterns; little boys envied his adroitness and fame. In the yard he was nicknamed the 'Mechanic.'

"Later in Petersburg, Ivan Babichev graduated from the Polytechnic Institute in the Mechanics Department, actually, the very same year his brother Roman was executed. Ivan worked as an engineer in Nikolayevo, near Odessa, at the Naval Factory, right up until the beginning of the European war.

"And there you have it..."

2

Bᴜᴛ ᴡᴀs he ever really an engineer?

The year the Two Bits was being built, Ivan was plying a trade that enjoyed little respect and was, for an engineer, simply disgraceful.

Imagine! He drew portraits at beer stands for people who asked for them, composed impromptu speeches on assigned topics, read palms, and demonstrated the power of his memory by repeating fifty random words read to him in a row.

Sometimes he would pull a deck of cards out of his shirt, which made him look instantly like a cardsharp, and do magic tricks.

People would buy him beer. He would take a seat and then the main event would begin: Ivan Babichev would prophesy.

What did he talk about?

"We are a breed of men that has reached its upper limit," he would say, banging his mug on the marble like a hoof. "Strong personalities, men who have decided to live their own way, egoists, obstinate men, I am turning to you as being more intelligent—my avant-garde! Listen those of you standing down front! An era is drawing to a close. The wave is breaking on the rocks, the wave is frothing, the foam is shimmering. What do you want? What? To vanish, to be reduced to nothing, droplets, a fine watery froth? No, my friends, you should not perish like that! No! Come to me, and I shall teach you."

His listeners paid him a certain respect but little attention, however they did support him with cries of "That's right!" and smatterings of applause. He would vanish without notice, pronouncing each time in farewell the same quatrain, which went like this:

No charlatan from Germany—
Deceit is not my game.
I'm a modern-day magician
With a Soviet claim to fame!

He also said the following:

"The gates are closing. Do you hear the gates creaking? Don't push. Don't try to penetrate beyond the threshold! Stop! Stopping is pride. Be proud. I am your leader, I am the king of the lowlifes. Anyone who sings and cries and smears his nose on the table when the beer is all drunk and they're not serving any more has a place here, by my side. Come, you who are heavy with grief, borne by song. You who kill out of jealousy, you who tie a noose for yourself—I'm calling on both of you, children of a lost era, come, you lowlifes and dreamers, you patresfamilias who dote on your daughters, honest philistines, loyal to tradition, obedient to the standards of honor, duty, and love, who fear blood and chaos, my dear ones—soldiers and generals—let us launch a campaign. Where? I shall lead you."

He devoured crabs. Crab carnage spilled from his hands. He was messy. His shirt, which looked like a tavern napkin, was always open at the chest. Not only that, but occasionally he would show up with starched cuffs, too. But dirty ones. If messiness can be combined with a tendency toward dandyism, then this would have suited him perfectly. For instance: the bowler. For instance: the flower in his buttonhole (which stayed there until it nearly formed fruit). And another for instance: the fraying trouser hems and the hanging threads of several long-gone jacket buttons.

"I'm a crab devourer. Look: I don't eat them, I destroy

them, like a priest. See? Marvelous crabs. Tangled up in sea-weed. Ah, not seaweed? Plain greens, you say? Does it matter? Let's call it seaweed. Then we can compare the crab to a ship raised from the bottom of the sea. Marvelous crabs. Kamsk crabs."

He licked his fist, looked up his cuff, and pulled out a crab shell.

Had he ever really been an engineer? Wasn't he lying? The picture of an engineer's soul, an affinity for machines, metal, and blueprints—it just didn't mesh with him! You would sooner take him for an actor or a defrocked priest. He was well aware that his listeners didn't believe him. He himself spoke with a certain twinkle in the corner of his eye.

First at one saloon, then another, the tubby prophet would appear. Once he went so far as to allow himself to clamber onto a table...Clumsy and in no way prepared for high jinks like that, he climbed over heads, clutching at palm leaves —breaking bottles, felling palms. He steadied himself on the table, and waving two empty mugs like dumbbells, began to shout, "Here I am standing on the heights, surveying my gathering army! Come to me! Come to me! Great is my host! Small-time actors dreaming of glory! Unlucky lovers! Old maids! Bookkeepers! Ambitious men! Fools! Knights! Cowards! Come to me! Your king has come, Ivan Babichev! The time is not yet come; soon, soon we shall advance... Gather around, my host!"

He flung the mug aside and grabbing a concertina out of someone's hands, spread it across his belly. The moan he extracted raised a storm: paper napkins flew up toward the ceiling.

Men in aprons and oilskin cuffs ran out from behind the counter.

"Beer! Beer! Give us more beer! Give us a keg of beer! We have to drink to great events!"

But they didn't serve any more beer, and the crowd was

pushed out into the dark, and they drove out the prophet Ivan—the smallest of them all, and heavy, which made it hard for them to escort him out. Stubbornness and rage suddenly gave him the dead weight of a steel barrel full of oil.

They pulled his bowler down shamefully around his ears.

He started down the street, staggering in various directions, as if he were being passed from hand to hand, and sang—or was he wailing?—piteously, embarrassing passersby.

"Ophelia!" he sang. "Ophelia!" Just that one word; it raced overhead, it seemed to fly above the streets in a quickly looping, shining figure eight.

That same night he visited his famous brother. The two sat at the table. One facing the other. In the middle of the table was the lamp under the green lampshade. His brother Andrei was sitting there and so was Volodya. Volodya was asleep, his head resting on his book. Ivan, drunk, headed for the sofa. For a long time he kept trying to pull the sofa under him, the way people pull up a chair.

"You're drunk, Vanya," said his brother.

"I hate you," replied Ivan. "You're an idol."

"Aren't you ashamed, Vanya? Lie down, go to sleep. I'll get you a pillow. Take off the bowler."

"You don't believe one word I say. You're a dolt, Andrei. Don't interrupt me. Otherwise I'll bust the lampshade over Volodya's head. Quiet. Why don't you believe in Ophelia's existence? Why don't you believe I invented a marvelous machine?"

"You didn't invent anything, Vanya. This is an obsession with you. You're making a bad joke. Aren't you ashamed of yourself, huh? After all, you're trying to take me for a fool. So what kind of a machine is this? Can there really be a machine like that? And why 'Ophelia'? And why do you wear a bowler? Are you an antiques dealer, a diplomatic envoy?"

Ivan was silent. Then, as if sobering up all at once, he rose, and clenching his fists, he walked toward his brother.

"You don't believe me? You don't? Andrei, stand up when the leader of an army of millions is talking to you. You have the nerve not to believe me? You say there's no such machine? Andrei, I promise you: that machine will be your downfall."

"Don't make a row," his brother replied. "You'll wake up Volodya."

"I spit on your Volodya. I know, I know your plans. You want to give Volodya my daughter. You want to rear a new breed. My daughter is not an incubator. You aren't going to get her. I won't give her to Volodya. I'll strangle her with my own hands."

He paused and with a twinkle in the corner of his eye, thrust his hands into his pockets, and sort of lifting his belly, which was poking out, with his hands, said in a tone dripping with malice, "You're mistaken, brother. You're pulling the wool over your own eyes. Oh ho, sweetie. You think you love Volodya because Volodya is a new man? Pish-tush, Andryusha. Pish-tush... That's not it, Andryusha, that's not it... Quite the contrary."

"What then?" asked Andrei ominously.

"You're just getting old, Andryusha. You just need a son. These are just fatherly feelings. The family—it's eternal, Andrei. And the idea of the new world being symbolized by the image of an unremarkable youth known only on the soccer field—it's nonsense..."

Volodya raised his head.

"Greetings Edison of the new day!" exclaimed Ivan. "Hurrah!" And he bowed extravagantly.

Volodya looked at him in silence. Ivan guffawed.

"What is it, Edison? Don't you believe there's an Ophelia either?"

"You, Ivan Petrovich, should be put in Kanatchikov," said Volodya, yawning.

Andrei gave a brief snort.

Then the prophet flung his bowler on the floor.

"Boors!" he exclaimed. And after a pause: "Andrei! You're allowing this? Why are you allowing your heir to insult your brother?"

Ivan did not see his brother's eyes; Ivan saw only a flash of glass.

"Ivan," said Andrei, "I beg of you never to come see me again. You're not insane. You're a beast."

3

DISCUSSIONS ensued about the new prophet.

From the saloons, a rumor ricocheted into apartments and crawled down the dark passages into the communal kitchens —in the hour of morning washing up, in the hour of primus stove lighting, people watching the milk trying to boil over and others splashing under the tap blathered gossip.

The rumor spread to institutions, rest homes, and markets.

A story was composed about a citizen, a stranger (who wore a bowler, according to the details, a shabby, suspicious man, none other than Ivan Babichev himself), who went to a wedding for a bill collector, on Yakimanka, and presenting himself at the very height of the feast, demanded everyone's attention for his speech—an address to the newlyweds. He said, "You don't have to love each other. You don't have to unite. Groom, leave your bride. What fruit will your love bear? You'll bring your own enemy into the world. He'll devour you."

The groom was ready to start a fight. The bride crumpled to the ground. The guests departed, greatly offended, whereupon it seems to have been discovered that the port wine in all the bottles on the feast table had turned to water.

Another amazing story was dreamed up.

It seems an automobile was driving through a very noisy place (some said Neglinny near Kuznetsky Bridge, others Tverskaya near the Monastery of the Passion), and in it sat a respectable citizen, stout, red-cheeked, holding a briefcase on his knees.

And apparently his brother Ivan, that same famous little

man, ran out from the crowd into the street. Envying his riding brother, he stood in the car's way, arms spread like a scarecrow, or the way people do when they stop a runaway horse by spooking it. The driver managed to slow down in time. He honked, continuing to inch forward, but the scarecrow wouldn't get out of the road.

"Stop!" the little man shouted at the top of his voice. "Stop, commissar! Stop, kidnapper of other people's children!"

The driver had no choice but to brake. Traffic came to a halt. Several vehicles nearly reared up as they flew at the car in front, and a bus gave a roar and stopped, utterly distraught, ready to surrender, to pick up its elephant tires and tiptoe back... The man standing in the street with outstretched arms demanded silence.

And everything fell silent.

"Brother," the little man intoned. "Why are you riding in an automobile while I go on foot? Open the door, move over, let me in. Going on foot doesn't suit me either. You're a leader, but I'm a leader, too."

And indeed, at these words people ran up to him from different sides, several jumped out of the bus, others left the nearby beer stands, still others hurried over from the boulevard—and the man sitting in the automobile, the brother, having stood up, immense, even bigger because he was standing in an automobile, saw before him a living barricade.

His ominous look was such that he seemed about to take a step and walk across the vehicle, across the driver's back, onto those at the barricade, like a crushing pillar—the full height of the street...

Ivan, meanwhile, had actually been lifted on people's arms: he rose above the crowd of disciples, swayed, fell down, and snapped back up; his bowler slipped back on his head, exposing the large, clear brow of a weary man.

And his brother Andrei dragged him down from that

height, grabbing a handful of his trousers at the belly. He flung him like that at a policeman.

"To the GPU!" he said.

Scarcely had the magic word been spoken than the crowd shook itself out of its stupor and emerged from its state of lethargy; matches sparked, plugs started spinning, doors slammed, and all the actions resumed that had begun before the lethargy.

Ivan was under arrest for ten days.

When he was returned to freedom, his friends and fellow drinkers asked him whether it was true he'd been arrested on the street by his brother and under such amazing circumstances. He guffawed.

"That's a lie. A legend. They just arrested me at a beer-stand. I think they've been watching me for a long time. But anyway, it's good they're already making up legends. The end of an era, a transitional period, needs its own legends and tales. I'm happy, you know, I'm going to be the hero of one of those tales. And there's going to be another legend: about the machine that bore the name 'Ophelia'... The era will die with my name on people's lips. That's what I'm applying my efforts to."

They let him go, threatening him with deportation.

What did they accuse him of at the GPU?

"Have you been calling yourself a king?" the investigator asked him.

"Yes... king of the lowlifes."

"What does that mean?"

"You see, I'm opening the eyes of a large category of people..."

"What are you opening their eyes to?"

"They have to understand that they're doomed."

"You said 'a large category of people.' Who do you have in mind by that category?"

"Everyone you call decadents. The bearers of decadent moods. If you will allow me, I'll elaborate."

"I would appreciate that."

"...a number of human emotions seem subject to extinction..."

"For example? Emotions like..."

"...pity, tenderness, pride, jealousy, love—in short, nearly all the emotions comprised by the soul of the man in the era now coming to a close. The era of socialism will create a new series of conditions for the human soul to replace the old emotions."

"I see."

"I see you understand me. A Communist bitten by the snake of jealousy is subject to persecution. So too is a compassionate Communist subject to persecution. The buttercup of pity, the lizard of ambition, the snake of jealousy—these flora and fauna must be driven out of the new man's heart.

"...please forgive me for speaking so eloquently, does it seem too flowery to you? Is it hard for you? Thank you. Water? No, I don't want water...I like speaking beautifully...

"...we know that the grave of a Young Communist who has laid hands on himself is adorned, among the wreathes, with the curses of his comrades-in-arms as well. The man of the new world says: Suicide is a decadent act. But a man of the old world said: He had to kill himself to save his honor. Thus we are saying that the new man is teaching himself to despise the old-fashioned emotions glorified by poets and the muse of history herself. Well, there you have it. And I want to organize a final parade of these emotions."

"Is this what you call the conspiracy of emotions?"

"Yes. This is the conspiracy of emotions, at the head of which I stand."

"Go on."

"Yes. I would like to organize a troupe around me...Are you following me?

"...you see, one can allow that the old-fashioned emotions were beautiful. Examples of great love, let's say, for a woman or the fatherland. Anything! You'll agree that some of these memories stir us even today. Isn't that true? So you see I would like...

"...you know, sometimes an electric lightbulb goes out all of a sudden. Fizzles, you say. And this burned-out bulb, if you shake it, it flashes again and it'll burn a little longer. Inside the bulb it's a disaster. The wolfram filaments are breaking up, and when the fragments touch, life returns to the bulb. A brief, unnatural, undeniably doomed life—a fever, a too-bright incandescence, a flash. Then comes the darkness, life never returns, and in the darkness the dead, incinerated filaments are just going to rattle around. Are you following me? But the brief flash is magnificent!

"I want to shake...

"...I want to shake the heart of a fizzled era. The lightbulb of the heart, so that the broken pieces touch...

"...and produce a beautiful, momentary flash...

"...I want to find representatives from there, from what you call the old world. The emotions I have in mind are jealousy, love for a woman, ambition. I want to find a foolish man to show you: Here, comrades, is a representative of that human condition known as foolishness.

"...many personalities played out the comedy of the old world. The curtain has fallen. The characters still have to run to the front of the stage and sing the final couplets. I want to be the intermediary between them and the viewing audience. I'll conduct the chorus and be last to leave the stage.

"...I have been given the honor of conducting the last parade of old-fashioned human passions...

"...through the eye slits of a mask, history is watching us with a flickering gaze. And I want to show it: Here is a man in love, here a man of ambition, here a traitor, here a reckless hero, here a loyal friend, here a prodigal son. Here they are, the bearers of great emotions that have now been deemed unimportant and vulgar. One last time, before they vanish, before they're laughed at, let them show themselves in their full intensity.

"...I'm listening to a strange conversation. They're talking about a razor. About a madman who slit his own throat. At that point a woman's name flits by. He didn't die, the madman, they stitched up his neck, and he slit it again in the exact same place. Who is he? Show him, I need him, I'm searching for him. And I'm searching for her. Her, the demonic woman, and him, the tragic lover. But where am I to search for him? At Sklifossovsky Hospital? And her? Who is she? A shopgirl? A nepman's wife?

"...I'm having a very hard time finding my heroes...

"...there are no heroes...

"...I look into other people's windows, go up other people's stairs. From time to time I run after someone else's smile, skipping, like a naturalist running after a butterfly! I feel like shouting: Stop! What's blossoming on the bush that shaky and precipitate moth of your smile flew out of? What's that bush's emotion? Is it the pink dog rose of sorrow, or the currant of petty ambition? Stop! I need you...

"...I want to gather a multitude around me. So that I have a choice and can choose the best, the most vivid of them, to form a shock troop, sort of...a shock troop of emotions.

"...yes, this is a conspiracy, a peaceful uprising. A peaceful demonstration of emotions.

"...let's say somewhere I find a full-blooded, 100 percent man of ambition. I'll say to him: Show yourself! Show those people who are wiping you out, show them what ambition is. Commit an act so that people can say, Oh, base ambition! Oh, what power ambition has! Or, let's say, if I'm so fortunate as to find an ideally frivolous man. I'll ask him, too: Show yourself, show the power of frivolity, make the spectators clap their hands.

"...the geniuses of emotions have power over men's souls. The genius of pride rules one soul, the genius of compassion another. I want to extract them, these demons, and release them in an arena."

Investigator: "So, have you managed to find anyone yet?"

Ivan: "I've been calling and searching for a long time. It's very hard. Maybe they don't understand me. But I did find one."

Investigator: "Who exactly?"

Ivan: "Are you interested in the emotion whose bearer he is or in his name?"

Investigator: "Both."

Ivan: "Nikolai Kavalerov. Envier."

4

THEY MOVED away from the mirror.

Now the two comics were walking together. One, shorter and fatter, was a step ahead of the other. This was a peculiarity of Ivan Babichev. As he conversed with his companion, he was constantly forced to look back. If he had a long sentence to say (and his sentences were never short), then frequently, as he strode, his face turned to his fellow traveler, he would bump into the people walking toward him. Then he would immediately tear off his bowler and dissolve in high-flown apologies. He was a courteous man. A welcoming smile never left his face.

The afternoon was rolling up the stalls. A gypsy in a dark blue vest, with painted cheeks and a beard, had hoisted a clean copper bowl on his shoulder. The afternoon was moving off on the gypsy's shoulder. The bowl's disk was bright and blind. The gypsy was walking slowly, the bowl was rocking gently, and the afternoon was spinning in its disk.

The fellow travelers watched it go.

And the disk set, like the sun. The day was done.

The fellow travelers immediately went into a beer stand.

Kavalerov told Ivan about how he had been driven out of his own home by an important man. He didn't name names. Ivan told him about the same thing. He, too, had been driven out by an important man.

"And you probably know him. Everyone knows him. It's my brother, Andrei Petrovich Babichev. Heard of him?"

Kavalerov blushed and looked down. He made no reply.

"In this way, our destiny is similar, and we should be friends," said Ivan, beaming. "And I like the name Kavalerov: it's highfalutin and low-down."

Kavalerov thought, "I'm highfalutin and low-down, too."

"Marvelous beer," exclaimed Ivan. "The Poles say, 'She has beer-colored eyes.' Nice, isn't it?

". . . but the main thing is that this famous man, my brother, stole my daughter from me . . .

". . . I'll make my brother pay.

". . . he stole my daughter from me. Well, he didn't literally steal her, naturally, don't make such big eyes, Kavalerov. And it wouldn't do you any harm to make your nose smaller, either. With a fat nose you have to be famous, like a hero, to be as happy as a common philistine. He exerted his moral influence on her. But can you sue him for that? Go to the prosecutor? Huh? She left me. I don't even blame Andrei as much as that swine who lives with him."

He was talking about Volodya.

Kavalerov's big toes were wiggling from embarrassment.

". . . that whippersnapper ruined my life. Oh, if only they'd kicked out his kidneys in soccer. Andrei listens to everything he says. He—that whippersnapper, you see—is the new man! That whippersnapper said Valya is unhappy because I, her father, am insane and that (the swine!) I am systematically driving her crazy. The swine! They ganged up to convince her. And Valya ran away. Some girlfriend took her in. I cursed that girlfriend. I said I wished her gullet and her gut would change places. Can you picture that? They're a bunch of numskulls . . .

". . . woman was the best, purest, most wonderful light of our culture. I sought a being of the female sex. I sought a kind of creature who combined all the feminine qualities. I sought the ovary of feminine qualities. The feminine was the glory of the old era. I wanted to shine like that feminine principle. We're dying, Kavalerov. I wanted to carry woman over my head like a torch. I thought that woman would die out along with our era. The millennia are like a cesspool. Floundering in the cesspool are machines, pieces of iron, tinplate, screws, springs... A dark and gloomy cesspool. And glowing in the cesspool are rotten stumps, phosphorescent mushrooms—fungi. These are our emotions! This is all that's left of our emotions, from the flourishing of our souls. The new man comes up to the cesspool, tests it, climbs in, picks out what he needs—a piece of a machinery will come in handy, a nice wrench—and tramples the rotten stump underfoot, crushes it. I dreamed of finding a woman who could flourish with unprecedented emotion in this cesspool. The miraculous blossoming of a fern. So that the new man who comes to steal our iron would take fright, pull his hand back, and shut his eyes, blinded by the light of what had seemed to him a rotten stump.

"...I found such a being. Right beside me. Valya. I thought Valya would shine over the dying era, light its way to the great graveyard. But I was wrong. She flitted away. She abandoned the tombstone of the old era. I thought woman was ours, that tenderness and love were only ours—but you see...I was wrong. And so I wander, the last dreamer on earth, along the edges of the cesspool, like a wounded bat..."

Kavalerov thought: "I'll tear Valya away from them." He felt like saying he had witnessed the incident in the lane where the garden bloomed. But for some reason he refrained.

"Our fates are similar," Ivan continued. "Give me your hand. I greet you. I'm very glad to see you, young man. Let's have a toast. So, you were driven out, Kavalerov? Tell me all about it. Actually, you already did. A very important man showed you the door? You don't want to name names? Well, all right. You hate this man very much."

Kavalerov nodded.

"Ah, how understandable I find all this, my good man! You, insofar as I've understood you, have had a caddish trick played on you by a powerful man. Don't interrupt me. You have come to despise a man recognized by all. You, of course, think that he has insulted you. Don't interrupt me. Drink.

"...you're certain that he's keeping you from making something of yourself, that he stole what was rightfully yours, that he reigns where, in your opinion, you should. And you're furious..."

An orchestra hovered in the smoke. The violinist's pale face was resting on his violin.

"The violin looks like the violinist himself," said Ivan. "It's a little violinist in a wooden tailcoat. Hear it? The wood's singing. Do you hear the wood's voice? The wood in an orchestra sings in different voices. But how miserably they play! God, how miserably they play!"

He turned around to face the musicians.

"Do you think that's a drum there? Do you think that's the drum playing its part? No, it's the god of music pounding you with his fist.

"...my friend, envy will swallow us up. We envy the coming era. If you like, we have here the envy of old age. We have here the envy of a human generation that has aged for the first time. Let's talk about envy. Give us some more beer..."

They were sitting next to a large window.

It was raining again. It was evening. The town glistened as if it had been chiseled out of Cardiff coal. People looked in the window from Samoteka, pressing their noses up.

"...yes, envy. Here a drama must unfold, one of those grandiose dramas in the theater of history that have inspired the lament, ecstasy, sympathy, and fury of mankind. Without even knowing it, you are a bearer of a historical mission. You are a clot, so to speak. A clot of envy in the dying era's bloodstream. The dying era envies the era that's coming to take its place."

"What can I do?" asked Kavalerov.

"My dear, here you must resign yourself or else...create a

scandal. Go out with a bang. Slam the door, as they say. That's the most important part: go out with a bang. Leave a scar on history's ugly face. Shine, damn it! They aren't going to let you in anyway. Don't give up without a fight...I want to tell you about an incident from my childhood.

"A gala had been arranged. Children acted out a play and performed a ballet on a stage built especially in a large drawing room. And a little girl...can you imagine her?—a very typical little girl, twelve years old, dainty feet, short dress, all pink, satin, and ruffles, well, you know, the whole shebang— with her chiffon and ribbons, she looked like the flower known as a snapdragon—a beauty, haughty, spoiled, shaking her curls—that's the kind of girl who was dancing at this ball. She was a queen. She did whatever she wanted, everyone admired her, everything flowed from her and everything was drawn to her. She danced better than anyone, sang, leaped, thought up games. The best presents went to her, the best candies, flowers, oranges, and praises...I was thirteen, a schoolboy. She was outshining me. But meanwhile I, too, was used to ecstatic cries. I, too, had been spoiled by admiration. In my class I was first, the record holder. I couldn't stand it. I caught her in the corridor and beat her, tore her ribbons, sent her curls flying, scratched her beautiful face. I grabbed her by the nape and rammed her forehead into a column a few times. At that moment I loved that girl more than life, I worshipped her—and hated her with every fiber of my being. By tearing up the beauty's curls, I thought I would disgrace her, dispel her rosiness, her glow, I thought I would correct the mistake everyone had made. But that's not what happened. The disgrace fell on me. I was driven out. However, my dear, they did talk about me all evening; and I did spoil the gala for them. They talked about me everywhere the little beauty appeared...Thus for the first time did I know envy. The horrible burning of envy. How hard it is to envy! Envy constricts your throat with a spasm, squeezes your eyes from their sockets. While I was tearing my victim to pieces there, in the corridor, tears rolled from my eyes, I was sobbing—and still I tore her exquisite clothing, trembling at the satin's touch, which left a bitter taste on my teeth and lips. You know what satin is, the texture of satin—you know how touching it sends a shiver running down your spine, through your whole nervous system, the grimaces it elicits! So all the powers rose up against me in defense of the nasty little girl. The bitter taste, the poison hidden in the bushes and baskets, flowed from what had seemed so enchanting in the drawing room— from her dress, from the pink satin, so sweet to the eyes. I remember emitting these cries while meting out my punishment. I was probably whispering, 'Here's your revenge! Don't try to outshine me! Don't take what might have belonged to me...'

"Have you been listening closely? I'm trying to draw an analogy. I have in mind the struggle between the eras. Naturally, at first glance the comparison will seem frivolous. But do you follow me? I'm talking about envy."

The orchestra finished its number.

"Well, thank God," said Ivan. "They've stopped. Look at the cello. It shone much less before they went after it. They tortured it for such a long time. Now it's shining as if it were wet—a spanking new cello. You should write down my opinions, Kavalerov. I'm not talking—I'm chiseling my words in marble. Aren't I?

"... my dear, we were record holders, we were spoiled by our generation, too, we were used to being first there, too ... at home ... where at home? ... There, in the dwindling era. Oh, how wonderful the rising world is, oh how the holiday they will not let us celebrate sparkles. Everything flows from this, the new era, everything is drawn to it, it will get the best gifts and exclamations. I love it, this world that's coming toward me, more than life, I worship it and hate it with every fiber of my being! I sob, tears gush from my eyes, but I want to poke my fingers in its clothes and rip. Don't outshine me! Don't take away what might have belonged to me.

"...we have to take our revenge. Both you and I—there are thousands and thousands of us—we have to take our revenge. Kavalerov, enemies are not always windmills. Sometimes what you'd like to take for a windmill is an enemy, a conqueror bearing death and destruction. Your enemy, Kavalerov, is a real enemy. Take your revenge on him. Believe me, we'll go out with a bang. We'll take the young world down a peg. We weren't born yesterday, either. We, too, have been history's darlings.

"...make people talk about you, Kavalerov. It's clear that everything is on its way to wrack and ruin, everything has been predetermined, there's no escape—you're going to perish, fat-nose! Every minute the humiliations are going to multiply, every day your enemy is going to flourish like a pampered youth. We're going to perish. That's clear. So dress up your demise, dress it up in fireworks, tear the clothes off whoever is outshining you, say farewell in such a way that your 'goodbye' comes crashing down through the ages."

Kavalerov thought, "He's reading my mind."

"Have you been insulted? Driven out?"

"I've been terribly insulted," said Kavalerov hotly. "I've been humiliated for a long time."

"Who insulted you? One of the era's chosen?"

"Your brother," Kavalerov wanted to shout, "the same one who insulted you." But he held his tongue.

"You're lucky. You know your conqueror's face. You have a concrete enemy. So do I."

"What should I do?"

"You're lucky. You can combine revenge for yourself with revenge for the era that was mother to you."

"What should I do?"

"Kill him. Leave behind an honorable memory of yourself as your era's hired assassin. Squeeze your enemy between one era and the next. He's strutting, he's already there, he's already a genius, a cupid trailing his suite at the gates of the new world—his nose is in the air and he doesn't see you—give him a good bang in parting. My blessings on you. And I"—Ivan raised his mug—"I, too, will destroy my enemy. Let's drink, Kavalerov, to Ophelia. She is the instrument of my revenge."

Kavalerov opened his mouth to tell him the most important thing: We have a common enemy, you've given me your blessing to kill your brother. But he didn't say a word because a man came up to their table and invited Ivan to follow him immediately, no questions asked. He was arrested, as we know from the preceding chapter.

"Goodbye, my dear," said Ivan. "They're taking me to Golgotha. Go see my little girl"—he named the lane that had shone for so long in Kavalerov's memory—"go there and look at her. You'll understand that if such a creation betrayed you, there would be only one thing left: revenge."

He finished his beer and walked one step ahead of the mysterious man.

On his way he winked at the customers, lavished smiles, glanced into the clarinet's bell, and right at the door turned around. Holding his bowler in his extended hand, he declaimed:

> No charlatan from Germany—
> Deceit is not my game.
> I'm a modern-day magician
> With a Soviet claim to fame!

5

"WHAT ARE you laughing for? You think I want to sleep?" asked Volodya.

"But I'm not laughing. I'm coughing."

And Volodya went back to sleep almost before he could reach the chair.

Young people got tired earlier. The other, older man—Andrei Babichev—was a giant. He worked all day and half the night. Andrei banged his fist on the table. The lampshade jumped up and down like the lid on a teakettle, but the other slept. The lampshade jumped. Andrei remembered James Watt watching the teakettle lid jumping over the steam.

A famous legend. A famous picture.

James Watt inventing the steam engine.

"What will you invent, my James Watt? What machine will you invent, Volodya? What new secret of nature will you uncover, new man?"

And at this Andrei Babichev began a conversation with himself. For a very short while he abandoned his work and, looking at the sleeping man, thought:

"Could Ivan be right? Maybe I'm just an ordinary philistine and the family principle lives on in me. Is this why he's so dear to me, this man who's been living with me since his childhood years? Am I just used to him, have I come to love him like a son? Is that the only reason? Is it that simple? And what if he turned out to be a dolt? What I live for is focused in him. I've been lucky. The life of the new man is a long way off. I believe in it. And I've been lucky. Here he's fallen asleep so close to me, my beautiful new world. The new world is living in my own house. I positively worship him. A son? A support? The grand finale of an era? That's not true! That's not what I need! I don't want to die on a high bed, on pillows. I know it's the masses, not a family, that will receive my last breath. Nonsense! We're coddling this new world the way I coddle him. He's precious to me as an embodied hope. I'll drive him out if I'm wrong about him, if he isn't new, isn't completely distinct from me, because I'm still up to my gut in the old and can't climb out anymore. I'll drive him away then. I don't need a son. I'm no father, he's no son, and we're no family. I'm the one who had faith in him, and he's the one who's justified my faith.

"We're no family, we're mankind.

"What does that mean? Does it mean the human emotion of fatherly love has to be destroyed? Why does he love me, he, the new man? This means that there, in the new world, the love between son and father will flourish as well. Then I do have the right to smile; then I do have the right to love him both as a son and as the new man. Ivan, Ivan, your conspiracy is pointless. Not all emotions are going to perish. Your rage is in vain, Ivan! Something will remain."

Long long ago, one dark night, swallowed by a ravine, up to their knees in stars, frightening the stars out of the shrubbery, two people were running: a commissar and a boy. The boy had saved the commissar. The commissar was huge, the boy a mite. Anyone who saw them would have thought that the giant, who kept falling to the ground, was fleeing, and they would have taken the boy for the giant's hand.

They had bonded forever.

The boy lived with the giant, grew, grew up, became a Young Communist, and went to the university. He'd been born in a railway village, the son of a linesman.

His comrades loved him, adults loved him. He sometimes worried that everyone liked him; sometimes this seemed unmerited and mistaken. Camaraderie was his strongest emotion. Concerned about balance, or, more precisely, the imbalance committed by nature in distributing gifts, he sometimes resorted to dodges to even out the impression he made, to lower it, anxious to dampen his own glow.

He wanted to reward other less successful people his age with his devotion, his readiness for self-sacrifice, his ardent manifestations of friendship, his search in each of them for remarkable traits and abilities.

His presence spurred his comrades to competition.

"I thought, why do people get angry or insulted?" he said. "People like that have no concept of time. This demonstrates their unfamiliarity with technology. Time is a technical concept, after all. If everyone were technicians, then hate, vanity, and all the petty emotions would vanish. You're smiling? You have to understand it. You need to understand time in order to be free of petty emotions. An insult might last, say, an hour or a year. They have enough imagination for a year. But they aren't going to have enough momentum for a thousand years. They see only three or four sections on the dial, they're crawling, fussing... Where can they go! They aren't going to cover the whole dial. And anyway, if you tell them there's a dial, they won't believe you!

"So why only petty emotions? Lofty emotions are short-lived too, after all. What about magnanimity?

"You see, you have to listen to what I'm saying. There's a correctness in magnanimity... a technical correctness. Don't smile. Yes, yes. No, in fact... I think I've got it mixed up. You're confusing me. No, wait up! The revolution was... well, what? Very cruel, of course. Hah! But who was it out to get? It was magnanimous, right? There was enough good for the whole dial! Right? You have to be insulted for the whole circle of the dial, not just two sections... Then there's no difference between cruelty and magnanimity. Then there's one thing: time. The iron logic of history, as they say. But history and time are one and the same, doubles. Don't laugh, Andrei Petrovich. I'm saying that man's main emotion has to be an understanding of time."

He also said, "I'll knock the bourgeois world down a peg. They're making fun of us. The old men are grumbling. Where are your new engineers, surgeons, professors, inventors? they say. I'll assemble a big group of comrades, a hundred or so. We'll organize a union. For taking the bourgeois world down a peg. You think I'm boasting? You don't understand anything. I'm not getting carried away at all. We're going to work like animals. Wait and see. People will come bow at our feet. And Valya's going to be in that union."

He woke up.

"I was dreaming," he laughed, "dreaming that Valya and I were sitting on a roof and looking at the moon through a telescope."

"What's that? Huh? A telescope?"

"And I'm telling her that way down there, below, is the 'sea of crises,' and she asks me, 'A sea of cries?'"

That spring Volodya went away for a while to visit his father in Murom. His father worked in the Murom locomotive-building shops. After two days of separation, on the night of the third day, Andrei was riding home. At a turn the driver slowed down, it was getting light, and Andrei saw a man lying at the base of a wall.

The man lying on the grate reminded him of the absent man. He jerked to attention at the sight and leaned toward the driver. "No, they have nothing in common," Andrei nearly cried out. And indeed, there was no similarity between the man lying there and the man who was absent. It was simple: he had a vivid picture of Volodya in his mind. He thought, "What if suddenly something compelled Volodya to adopt the same pathetic pose? It was simple; he'd done

YURI OLESHA

something foolish and let his emotions run wild." The car stopped.

They lifted Nikolai Kavalerov up and listened to his ravings.

Andrei brought him home, dragged him to the fourth floor and put him to bed on Volodya's sofa, tucked him in, and pulled the blanket up to his neck. He lay there on his back, the grating's waffle impression still on his cheek. His host walked off to bed in a state of contentment: the sofa was not going empty.

That same night, he dreamed that a young man had hanged himself on a telescope.

6

THERE was a remarkable bed in Anichka Prokopovich's room. It was made of precious wood with a dark cherry varnish and had mirrored arches on the inside of the headboard.

One day, in a peaceful year long past, on a national holiday, to a fanfare, sprinkled with confetti, Anichka's husband climbed a wooden platform, showed his lottery ticket, and received from the master of ceremonies a receipt giving him the right to own the marvelous bed. They carted it away. Little boys whistled. The blue sky was reflected in the moving mirrored arches, like the lids on two beautiful eyes opening and slowly closing.

The family lived and fell apart—and the bed made it through all the bad times.

Now Kavalerov lived in the corner behind the bed.

He had gone to see Anichka and said, "Thirty rubles a month, that's what I can pay you for that corner."

And Anichka smiled broadly and agreed. He had nowhere else to go. A new tenant was firmly ensconced in his old room. Kavalerov sold his terrible bed for four rubles, and it moaned and groaned leaving him.

Anichka's bed looked like an organ.

It took up half the room. Its top faded into the twilight of the ceiling.

Kavalerov thought, "If I were a child, Anichka's little son, just think how many poetic, magical notions my childish mind would create in thrall to the spectacle of this extraordinary thing! Now I'm an adult, and now I can only pick out its general outlines, a few details here and there, but then I could have...

"...But then, surrendering neither to distances, nor scales, nor time, nor weight, nor gravity, I would have crawled in the corridors formed by the gap between the bedspring and the bedframe; I would have hidden behind the columns that now seem no bigger than measuring glasses; I would have set imaginary catapults on its barriers and fired at my enemies losing strength in their flight across the soft, sucking ground of the blanket; I would have arranged receptions for ambassadors under the mirrored arch, like the king of the novel I'd just read; I would have embarked on fantastic journeys over the carving—up and up—over the cupids' legs and buttocks, I would have crawled over them the way people crawl over the statue of the Buddha, unable to take it in with one glance, and from the last arch, from that dizzying height, I would have hurled myself into the terrible abyss, into the pillows' icy abyss..."

Ivan Babichev was leading Kavalerov over a green mound ...Dandelions were flying out from under his feet, sailing— and their sailing was a dynamic reflection of the heat... Babichev was pale from the heat. His full face was shining; the heat was actually carving a mask from his face.

"Over here!" he commanded.

The outskirts of town were in bloom.

They crossed a vacant lot and walked along the fences. German shepherds raged behind the fences and rattled their chains. Kavalerov whistled, taunting the dogs. But anything's possible: a dog might get smart, break its chain, bound over the fence. A capsule of terror dissolved somewhere in the pit of the taunter's stomach.

The companions went down a greening slope, nearly onto the roofs of the little red houses at the top of the gardens. Kavalerov didn't know the place, and even when he saw the Krestovsky water towers in front of him, he couldn't get oriented. The whistling of locomotives, the railroad clang, reached him.

"I'll show you my machine," said Ivan, glancing back at Kavalerov. "You'll pinch yourself...okay...again...and again...It's not a dream? No? Remember, you weren't sleeping. Remember, it was all very simple: you and I walked across a vacant lot, a puddle that never dries up shone, there were pots on the paling—remember that, my friend—there were remarkable things to notice in the trash along the way, under the fences, in the gutters; for instance, look, a page from a book. Bend down, take a look before the wind carries it away. See? An illustration from *Taras Bulba*—recognize it?—they probably threw out the wrapping from something to eat from that window, and the page landed here. Onward! What's this? Russia's eternal, traditional bast sandal in the gutter? Not worth noticing—too academic an image of desolation! Onward! A bottle—wait, it's still whole, but tomorrow a cart wheel will crush it, and if soon after us some other dreamer comes our way, he'll have the perfect satisfaction of recognizing the famous bottle gas, the famous shards writers have glorified for their quality of blazing up amid the trash and desolation and creating all kinds of mirages for lonely wanderers. Observe, my friend, observe—over there, buttons, hoops, there's a scrap of bandage, there are little towers of Babel of petrified human feces...In short, my friend, the usual wasteland relief...Remember it. It was all simple. And I brought you here to show you my machine. Pinch yourself. Okay. That means you're not dreaming, right? Well, all right. But later—I know what's going to happen—later you're going to say you weren't feeling well, it was too hot, you may have just imagined a lot of it because of the heat, the exhaustion, and so forth...No, my friend, I demand that you confirm that you are in a normal condition. What you are about to see may knock you for a loop."

Kavalerov confirmed it: "I am in the most normal condition."

There was a fence, a not very tall wooden fence.

"There she is," said Ivan. "Wait a second. Let's sit. Over here, above the gully. I was telling you that my dream was the machine to end all machines, a universal machine. I thought about the perfect instrument, I was figuring on concentrating hundreds of different functions in one small apparatus. Yes, my friend. A beautiful, noble task. A task worth getting fanatic over. I had the idea of subduing the mastodon of technology, making it tame, domestic...Of giving man a simple, familiar lever that wouldn't frighten him, that would be as ordinary as a doorknob..."

"I don't understand anything about mechanics," Kavalerov said. "I'm afraid of machines..."

"And I succeeded. Listen to me, Kavalerov. I invented just such a machine."

(The fence beckoned and, actually, one could easily assume there wasn't any secret behind its ordinary gray boards.)

"She can blow up mountains. She can fly. She can lift heavy weights. She can mine ore. She can take the place of a hot plate, a stroller, long-range weapons...This is the genius of mechanics itself..."

"Why are you smiling, Ivan Petrovich?"

(Ivan winked with the corner of his eye.)

"I'm blossoming. I can't talk about her without my heart leaping like an egg in boiling water. Listen to me. I gave her hundreds of abilities. I invented a machine that can do everything. Do you understand? You'd be about to see it, but..."

He stood up, and placing his hand on Kavalerov's shoulder, said solemnly, "But I forbade her. One fine day I realized I'd been given a supernatural opportunity to take revenge for my era...I'd corrupted the machine. On purpose. Out of spite."

He burst into happy laughter.

"No, you have to understand, Kavalerov, what a great satisfaction it is. I gave the basest of human emotions to the greatest creation of technology! I disgraced the machine. I took revenge for my era, which gave me the brain that lies in my skull, my brain, which dreamed up an amazing machine ...Who should I leave her to? The new world? They're chewing us up like food; they're bewitching the nineteenth century the way a boa bewitches a hare...Chewing us up and digesting us. What's useful they absorb, what's harmful they excrete...They excrete our emotions, our technology they absorb! I'm taking revenge for our emotions. They won't get my machine, they won't exploit me, they won't absorb my brain...My machine could have made the new era happy, just like that, from the very first days of its existence, brought technology into its heyday. But you see—they aren't going to get her! My machine is the dying era's way of giving the finger to the nascent age. They'll be drooling when they see her...Just think, the machine is their idol, the machine ...and all of a sudden...And all of a sudden the best machine of all turns out to be a liar, a lowlife, a sentimental good-for-nothing! Let's go...I'll show you...She can do anything, but right now she sings our ballads, the foolish ballads of the old era, and gathers the old era's flowers. She falls in love, gets jealous, cries, dreams...I did this. I mocked the divinity of these coming men, I mocked the machine. And I gave her the name of a girl who went out of her mind from love and despair—Ophelia...The most human and touching name of all..."

Ivan led Kavalerov along.

Ivan slipped through a gap, displaying to Kavalerov a shiny brassy backside—like two peas in a pod—two dumbbells. Maybe the heat really was having an effect on him, the unusual remote emptiness, the newness of the landscape, surprising for Moscow, maybe exhaustion really was taking its toll, except that when Kavalerov was left alone in that deserted place far removed from the legitimate noises of the city, he surrendered to a mirage, an auditory hallucination. It was as if he were hearing Ivan's voice talking to someone through the gap. Then Ivan recoiled. And Kavalerov did the same, even though he was standing a goodly distance from Ivan—as if fright were hiding somewhere in the trees opposite and was holding both of them on a single string that it was pulling.

"Who's whistling?" cried Kavalerov in a voice ringing with fear.

A piercing whistle soared over the immediate area. Kavalerov turned away for a second, hiding his face in his hands, the way people turn away from a draft. Ivan ran from the fence to Kavalerov, his little feet shuffling quickly; the whistle flew after him. Ivan seemed to be sliding, not running, strung on a blinding whistle ray.

"She scares me! She scares me!" Kavalerov heard Ivan's gasping whisper.

Grabbing hands, they ran downhill to the curses of an alarmed tramp whom at first, from high above, they'd taken for an old harness someone had thrown away.

The tramp, torn from sleep in one fell swoop, was sitting on a hummock, rifling through the grass—looking for a rock. They turned down a lane and were gone.

"She scares me," said Ivan quickly. "She hates me...She betrayed me...She's going to kill me..."

Once Kavalerov came to his senses, he was ashamed of his cowardice. He remembered that when he saw Ivan turn tail and run something else rose up in his field of vision, something he was too scared to let leave an impression.

"Listen," he said, "what rubbish! It was just a boy whistling on two fingers. I saw him. A boy popped up on the fence and whistled... Yeah, a boy..."

"I told you," Ivan smiled, "I told you you'd start looking for all kinds of explanations. And I begged you to pinch yourself harder."

They argued. Ivan went into the beer stand he finally found. He didn't invite Kavalerov to go with him. Kavalerov wandered, not knowing the way, searching for the sound of a tram. But at the next corner Kavalerov stamped his foot and went into the beer stand. Ivan greeted him with a smile and a hand pointing to a chair.

"So tell me," Kavalerov implored. "Answer me, why are you torturing me? Why are you trying to trick me? There isn't any machine, you see! There can't be any such machine! It's a lie, a delusion! Why are you lying to us?"

Exhausted, Kavalerov lowered himself into a chair.

"Listen, Kavalerov. Order yourself a beer, and I'll tell you a tale. Listen."

THE TALE OF TWO BROTHERS MEETING

The Two Bits' delicate, growing frame was surrounded by a forest.

A forest of, well, beams, tiers, staircases, entrances, passageways, and awnings, but in the crowd gathered at its base the personalities and eyes were all different. People smiled in variously similar ways. Some inclined to simplicity said that the structure was cross-hatched.

Someone else commented, "A wooden structure isn't supposed to rise too high. The eye doesn't respect boards that rise too high. Forests diminish a structure's grandeur. The very tallest mast seems so easy to snap. That hulk of wood is vulnerable, no matter what. You immediately wonder about a fire."

Someone else exclaimed, "On the other hand, look! Beams stretched out like strings! Just like a guitar—a guitar!"

To which the previous one commented: "Well, you

see, I was talking about the wood's vulnerability. Its fate is to serve music."

Then someone's mocking voice interjected, "What about the brass? I for one recognize only wind instruments."

A schoolboy saw in the distribution of the boards an arithmetic no one had noticed. But he never managed to determine what the crosses of multiplication referred to or where the equal signs led; the resemblance vanished in an instant. It was too shaky.

"The siege of Troy," thought the poet. "Siege towers."

And the comparison was reinforced by the appearance of the musicians. Hiding behind their horns, they crawled down a kind of wooden trench to the base of the structure.

The night was black, the lamps white and spherical, the panels unusually red, the gaps under the wooden gangways deathly black. The lamps swung, their chains clanking. The shadow seemed to wag its eyebrows. Around the street lamps a swarm of midges flew up and perished. From far away, making the windows along the way wink, the outlines of outlying houses torn off by street lamps flew past and rushed at the structure—and then (until the windblown lamp calmed down) the forest came to stormy life. Everything was set in motion, and like a triple-decker sailing ship, the structure sailed toward the crowd.

Andrei Babichev walked across wood and onto wood to the base of the structure. A podium had been built there. The orator had been given a staircase, and a platform, and a handrail, and a light that blinded the black backdrop—behind and directly above him. There was so much light that even distant observers could see the water level in the pitcher on the presidium's table.

Babichev moved above the crowd, very much in

color, and shining as if he were made of tin, like a little electric figure. He was supposed to give a speech. Below, in their naturally formed shelter, the actors were preparing for their performance. A hobo, invisible and incomprehensible to the crowd, began to wail sweetly. Incomprehensible, too, was the disk of the drum, which was turned to face the crowd and which the harshness of the lighting made silver. In their wooden canyon, the actors put on their makeup. Each step of the man striding overhead shook the boards above, sprinkling them with a haze of sawdust.

Babichev's appearance on the podium cheered the audience up. He was taken for the master of ceremonies. He was too fresh, deliberate, and theatrical in his appearance.

"Fat! Look how fat he is!" one man in the crowd admired.

"Bravo!" the shout went up in various places.

But "The floor goes to Comrade Babichev" was announced from the presidium—and the joking vanished without a trace. Many stood on tiptoe. Their attention strained. And everyone felt good. It felt very good to see Babichev for two reasons: first, he was a famous man; and second, he was fat. Fatness made the famous man one of them. They gave Babichev an ovation. Half of the applause was for being fat. He gave his speech.

He talked about what the Two Bits was going to do— how many meals, what capacities it would have, what percentage of nutrition—and the benefits of communal dining.

He talked about the feeding of children—that at the Two Bits, he said, there would be a children's section— about the scientific preparation of the milk porridge, about children's growth, the spine, anemia. Like any orator, he looked into the distance, over the heads of the audience down front, and so to the very end of his speech remained indifferent to what was going on below him, under the podium. But meanwhile a little man in a bowler had already long been distracting the spectators in front; they had stopped listening to the orator, riveted by the conduct of the little man who, actually, was being perfectly peaceable. True, he had taken a risk by leaving the crowd, clambering over the rope between him and the podium; true, he was standing apart, which obviously demonstrated he had certain rights, which either belonged to him or else he had simply usurped ...He was standing with his back to the audience and leaning on the rope, or, rather, half sitting on the rope, hanging his backside across it, and oblivious to the total chaos that would ensue if the rope broke, as calm as calm could be, and evidently deriving great pleasure from swinging there.

He may have been listening to the orator, or, possibly, observing the actors. The ballerina's dress flew up behind the crossbars, and all kinds of funny faces peered through the little wooden window.

And—yes! The main thing, after all, was what? He, this eccentric little man, had brought along a pillow. He was carrying a big old pillow in a yellowed pillowcase that had been slept on by many heads. And after he had settled on the rope, he lowered the pillow to the ground, and the pillow sat there next to him, like a pig.

When the orator finished his speech, he wiped his lips with his handkerchief with one hand and poured himself water from the pitcher with the other, and while the applause was dying down and the audience turned their attention, prepared to listen and watch the actors, the man with the pillow, lifting his backside off the rope, stood at his full short height, stretched out his arm with the pillow, and declaimed loudly, "Comrades! I would like to speak!"

Then the orator saw his brother Ivan. His fists clenched. His brother Ivan started going up the stairs to the podium. He ascended slowly. The man from the presidium ran toward the barrier. He was supposed to stop the stranger by his gestures and voice. But his hand hung in the air, and his arm dropped in jerks, exactly as if he were counting the stranger's steps up the stairs.

"One...two...five...ive..."

"It's hypnosis!" people in the crowd screamed.

The stranger was walking and carrying his pillow by the nape. And there he was on the podium. A remarkable, electric little figure appeared on the black backdrop. The backdrop was black as slate. The backdrop was so black, people imagined chalk lines there—they flickered in people's eyes. The little figure halted.

"The pillow!" the whisper ran through the crowd.

And the stranger began:

"Comrades! They want to take away your principal wealth: your home and hearth. The steeds of revolution, thundering up the black staircases, crushing your children and your cats, smashing your beloved hot plates and bricks, want to burst into your kitchens. Women! Your pride and glory—your hearth—is under attack. Mothers and wives, they want to smash your kitchens with the elephants of revolution!

"What was he saying? He was mocking your pans, your kettles, your stewpots, your right to stick your nipple between your baby's lips...He's teaching you to forget—what? What does he want to push out of your heart? The family home—your home, your dear home! He wants to turn you into tramps across the savage fields of history. Wives, he spits in your soup. Mothers, he dreams of wiping your babies' resemblance to you—

the sacred, beautiful family resemblance—off their little faces. He's breaking into your nooks and crannies,
scurrying like a rat over the shelves, he's crawling under the beds, under the nightshirts, in the hair of your
armpits. Drive him into Hell!...Here is a pillow. I am
the king of pillows. Tell him: Each of us wants to sleep
on his own pillow. Don't touch our pillows! Our still
unfledged heads, as rusty as chicken feathers, lay on
these pillows, our kisses fell on them in a night of love,
we died on these—and the people we killed died on
them, too. Don't touch our pillows! Don't summon us!
Don't lure us, don't tempt us! What can you offer to replace our ability to love, hate, hope, cry, regret, and forgive?...Here is a pillow. Our coat of arms. Our banner.
Here is a pillow. Bullets get stuck in pillows. We'll use
our pillow to smother you..."

His speech broke off. He had said too much as it was.
It was as if he'd been seized by his last phrase, the way
you can be seized by the arm: his phrase was bent behind his back. He stopped short, suddenly frightened,
and the real reason for his fright was that the man he
was fulminating against was standing there in silence,
listening. The whole scene could actually have been
taken for a performance. That's how many did take it.
Actors often do appear from the audience, after all.
Especially since the real actors were drifting out of the
wooden shed. Yes, like nothing so much as a butterfly
the ballerina flitted out from under the boards. An eccentric in a gorilla suit climbed onto the podium, grabbing onto the crossbar with one hand and with the
other holding an odd-looking instrument—a very long
horn with three bells. And since you could expect anything from a man in a gorilla suit and a red wig, the impression was easily formed of him climbing by some
magical means up that very same pipe. Someone in a

tailcoat was dashing about under the podium, trying to corral the scattering actors, who were struggling to see this extraordinary orator. You see, the actors, too, assumed that one of the showmen invited to participate in the concert had come up with a stunt, had brought along a pillow, had got into an argument with the speaker, and now his usual number would begin. But no. In terror, the eccentric slid down that idiotic pipe! Alarm began to spread. But it wasn't the words the stranger had scattered so luxuriantly on the crowd that sowed the disturbance. On the contrary, the little man's speech was perceived as intentional, a stunt. Now the ensuing silence raised the hairs under many caps.

"Why are you looking at me like that?" asked the little man, dropping the pillow.

The giant's voice (no one knew that this was brother talking to brother), the giant's brief cry was heard by the entire square, the windows, the entryways. Old men sat up in bed.

"Who are you fighting, scoundrel?" asked the giant.

His face crumpled. His face was leaking like a wineskin, from everywhere—his nostrils, lips, ears—some kind of dark liquid was oozing from his eyes, and everyone shut their own eyes in horror...But he hadn't said this. The boards around him had, the concrete, the braces, the lines, the formulas, which had taken on flesh. It was their fury that was bursting him open.

But his brother Ivan did not retreat (everyone was actually expecting him to retreat and retreat and plop down on his own pillow). On the contrary. Suddenly he found his strength, straightened up, walked toward the barrier, put his hand over his eyes like a visor, and called out, "Where are you? I'm waiting for you! Ophelia!"

A wind blew up. There had been gusts, actually, the

whole time, and the lamps had been swaying... Those present were by now used to the shadow figures (rectangles, Pythagorean trousers, Hippocratic crescents) combining and disintegrating—a triple-decker sailing ship of a structure was steadily breaking free of its mooring and advancing on the crowd—so that the new gust from which many shoulders turned and many heads bowed would have been met by ordinary displeasure and immediately forgotten had it not been for...

Afterward people said it flew up from behind and over their heads.

The huge ship sailed at the crowd, wood creaking, wind howling, and the black flying body—like a bird against the rigging—struck a tall beam and came crashing down, smashing a lamp.

"Scared, brother?" asked Ivan. "Here's what I'll do. I'll hurl her at your forest. She's going to destroy your structure. The screws will unscrew themselves, the nuts will fall off, the concrete will crack like a leprous body. All right? She'll teach every beam how to disobey you. All right? It's all going to come down. She's going to turn every number of yours into a useless flower. Here, brother Andrei, is what I can do..."

"Ivan, you're seriously ill. You're raving, Ivan," the man they'd been expecting storms from spoke gently and sincerely. "Who are you talking about? Who is 'she'? I don't see anything! Who is going to turn my figures into flowers? The wind just knocked a lamp against a beam, the lamp just broke. Ivan, Ivan..."

And his brother took a step toward Ivan and reached out. But Ivan fended him off.

"Look!" he cried, raising his hand. "No, you're not looking the right way... There, there... more to the left ...Do you see? What's that sitting there, on the beam? See? Drink some water. Pour Comrade Babichev some water... What's that perched there on the pole? Do you see?!! Do you believe?!! Are you afraid?!!"

"It's a shadow!" said Andrei. "Brother, it's just a shadow. Let's get out of here. I'll give you a ride. Let the show begin. The actors are tired of waiting. The public is waiting. Let's go, Vanya, let's go..."

"A shadow, is it? It's no shadow, Andryusha. It's the machine you've been laughing at... That's me sitting on the pole, Andryusha, me, the old world, my era is sitting there. The mind of my era, Andryusha, which knew how to compose both songs and formulas. A mind full of dreams, which you want to destroy."

Ivan raised his hand and shouted, "Go on, Ophelia! I'm ordering you!"

And then, after perching on the beam, it flashed on and off as it turned, spun, rattled, and stamped like a bird, and vanished into the dark gap between the crossed boards.

There was panic, a stampede, people were fleeing, howling. But it crawled along, making its way across the boards. Suddenly it peered out again, emitting a ray of orange light, and whistled something; elusive in shape, like a weightless shadow, spiderlike, it leaped perpendicularly, higher, into the chaos of boards, and again perched on an edge, and looked around...

"Do it, Ophelia! Do it!" shouted Ivan, racing around the podium. "Did you hear what he was saying about the hearth? I order you to destroy the building..."

People were fleeing, and their flight was accompanied by the flight of the clouds and a stormy fugue in the sky.

The Two Bits came crashing down...

The storyteller fell silent...

"A drum lay flat amid the ruins, and I, Ivan Babichev,

scrambled onto it. Ophelia hurried toward me, dragging the trampled, dying Andrei.

"'Lower me onto the pillow, brother,' he whispered. 'I want to die on a pillow. I surrender, Ivan...'

"I put the pillow on my knee, and he leaned his head against it.

"'We won, Ophelia,' I said."

7

SUNDAY morning Ivan Babichev paid a visit to Kavalerov.

"Today I want to show you Valya," he said with great ceremony.

They headed out. Their stroll could have been called enchanting. It was made through an empty, festive town. They circled around Theater Square. There was almost no traffic. The ascent up Tverskaya was blue. Sunday morning—one of the best views of a Moscow summer. The lighting, not fragmented by traffic, remained intact, as if the sun had just risen. In this way they walked along the geometric planes of light and shadow or, rather, through a stereoscopic body, because the light and shadow intersected not only along the plane but in the air as well. Before they reached the Moscow City Council building, they found themselves in full shadow. But in a gap between two bodies a large mass of light fell. It was thick, almost corporeal: here you could no longer doubt that light was tangible. The dust hanging in it could have passed for the oscillation of the ether.

And here was the lane connecting Tverskaya and Nikitskaya. They stood there admiring a blooming garden.

They went through some gates and up a wooden staircase to a glassed-in gallery that was deserted but made cheerful by its abundance of windows and the view of the sky through the lattice of windowpanes.

The sky was broken up into layers of varying blueness and proximity to the spectator. One window in four was smashed. The green tendrils of some plant climbed up of the gallery wall and in through the bottom row of windows. Everything here had been calculated for a cheerful childhood. Rabbits are raised in galleries like these.

Ivan headed for the door. There were three doors in the gallery. He was walking toward the last.

As he walked, Kavalerov felt like plucking one of the green tendrils. No sooner did he tug, though, than the entire invisible system outside was pulled by the tendril, and somewhere some wire entangled in the life of this ivy moaned, or the devil knows what (as if this were Italy, not Moscow...). Pressing his temple against the window and straining, Kavalerov saw a yard surrounded by a stone wall. The gallery was high up, halfway between the third and fourth floors. From that vantage he glimpsed before him, on the other side of the wall (more Italy), a view of a strange green yard.

When he stepped onto the stairs he heard voices and laughter. They came from that yard. Before he could figure out what was what, Ivan pulled him away. He knocked at the door. Once, twice, again...

"No one's here," he bellowed. "She's already there..."

Kavalerov's attention was still on the broken window above the lawn. Why? After all, so far nothing surprising had passed before his eyes. After turning toward Ivan's knock, he picked up just one patch of colorful movement, one stroke of gymnastic rhythm. It was simply that the green of the lawn, surprising after the ordinary yard, had been pleasant, sweet, and cool to the eye. More than likely, he later assured himself, he'd been gripped by the lawn's spell from the very start.

"She's gone!" Babichev repeated. "Please..."

And he looked out one of the little windows. Kavalerov did not hesitate to do the same.

What he'd thought was a lawn turned out to be a small yard grown up with grass. The main green impact came from the tall, heavily crowned trees around its sides. All this greenery was flourishing under the building's massive, blind wall.

Kavalerov was an observer from above. In his perception the yard was cramped. Everything around it stretched out beyond his high observation point and piled up above the yard, which lay there like a mat in a room full of furniture. Strangers' roofs revealed their secrets to Kavalerov. He saw a life-sized weathervane, dormer windows no one below even suspected, and a child's ball that had once flown too high and rolled under a gutter, never to be retrieved. Buildings bristling with antennae retreated up the steps from the yard. A church dome freshly painted in red lead popped up in an empty patch of sky, as if it had been flying around until Kavalerov caught it with his glance. He saw the rocking shaft of a trolley mast from a street at the back of beyond, and some other observer, who had stuck his head out of a distant window and was sniffing or eating something, vanquished by the view, was practically leaning on that rocking shaft.

But the yard was the main thing.

They went downstairs. In the stone wall that separated the big and little yards, the boring deserted yard from the mysterious lawn, there turned out to be a breach. A few stones were missing, like loaves pulled from an oven. Through this embrasure they saw everything. The sun seared the top of Kavalerov's head. They saw vaulting exercises. A rope had been strong between two columns. A youth flew up, carried his body over the rope sideways, almost sliding, stretched out parallel to the obstacle—as if he didn't jump but rolled over the obstacle, like over a mound. And as he rolled over it he kicked his legs out and they moved him along like a swimmer pushing at the water. In the next split second his distorted, thrown-back face flashed by, flying down, and then Kavalerov saw him standing on the ground. Moreover, when he hit the ground, he emitted a sound, sort of an "oof"—not quite a truncated exhalation, not quite his heels striking the grass.

Ivan pinched Kavalerov's elbow.

"There she is . . . look . . ." (in a whisper).

Everyone was shouting and clapping. The vaulter, who was nearly naked, stepped to one side, favoring one leg, probably an athlete's way of showing off.

It was Volodya Makarov.

Kavalerov was distraught. He was overcome by shame and fear. Volodya revealed a full, gleaming gearbox of teeth when he smiled.

Up above, in the gallery, someone was knocking at the door again. Kavalerov turned around. It had been very foolish to stop here, by the wall, to peep. Someone was walking through the gallery. The windows dismembered the walker. The parts of his body were moving independently. It was an optical illusion. The head was overtaking the torso. Kavalerov recognized the head. Andrei Babichev was sailing through the gallery.

"Andrei Petrovich!" Valya shouted on the lawn. "Andrei Petrovich! Over here! Over here!"

The terrible visitor vanished. He was leaving the gallery, searching for the way to the lawn. Various barriers hid him from Kavalerov's eyes. Time to flee.

"Over here! Over here!" Valya's voice rang out.

Kavalerov saw Valya standing on the lawn, her legs planted firmly and widely apart. She was wearing black trousers rolled up high; her legs were very bare, the whole structure of her legs was on display. She was wearing white sports shoes on bare feet, and because the shoes had flat heels her stance seem even firmer and solider—not a woman's but a man's or a child's. Her legs were spattered, tanned, gleaming. These were the legs of a girl that had felt the effect of air, sun, falling on hummocks, on grass, and blows so often that they were coarsened, covered with waxy scars from scabs pulled off too soon, and their knees were rough, like oranges. Their possessor's age and quiet confidence in her physical wealth gave her the right to be careless about her legs: she didn't spare them or pamper them. But higher, under her black trousers, the purity and softness of her body showed how lovely the possessor of these legs would be as she matured and became a woman, when she did pay attention to herself and did want to adorn herself—when the scabs healed, all the roughness fell away, and the sunburn evened out into a tan.

He pushed back from the embrasure and ran away along the blind wall, soiling his shoulder on the stone.

"Where are you going!" Ivan called him. "Where are you going! Where are you off to, wait up!"

"He's shouting loudly! They'll hear!" Kavalerov was horrified. "They'll see me!"

Indeed, it became abruptly quiet on the other side of the wall. They were listening. Ivan caught up to Kavalerov.

"Listen, my dear man ... Did you see? That's my brother! Did you see? Volodya, Valya ... Everyone! The whole camp ... Wait up, I'm going to climb the wall and give them a piece of my mind ... You're all dirty, Kavalerov, like a miller!"

Kavalerov said softly, "I know your brother very well. He's the one who drove me out. He's the important person I've been telling you about ... Our fates are analogous. You said I should kill your brother ... What should I do?"

Valya was sitting on the stone wall.

"Papa!" she exclaimed, gasping.

Ivan grabbed her by her feet, which were dangling from the wall.

"Valya, poke my eyes out. I want to be blind," he said, gasping. "I don't want to see anything: no lawns, no branches, no flowers, no knights, no trousers. I need to be blinded, Valya. I was wrong, Valya ... I thought the emotions had perished—love and devotion and tenderness, but it's all still here, Valya ... Only not for us, all that's left for us is envy and more envy ... Poke out my eyes, Valya, I want to go blind ..."

His arms, face, and chest slipped down the girl's sweaty legs, and he fell with a thud at the base of the wall.

"Let's drink, Kavalerov," said Ivan. "Let's drink, Kavalerov, to the youth that's past, to the conspiracy of emotions,
which has failed, to the machine, which never was and never
will be..."

"You're a son of a bitch, Ivan Petrovich!" Kavalerov
grabbed Ivan by the collar. "My youth isn't over! No! Do you
hear me? That's not true! I'll prove it to you... Tomorrow—
hear me?—tomorrow at the soccer match I'm going to kill
your brother..."

8

NIKOLAI Kavalerov took his seat in the stands. Up top, to his right, in a wooden box, between the panels, a sign in giant type, the short flights of stairs, and the crisscrossed boards, sat Valya. Young people were filling the box.

The day was bright and breezy, and the wind was whistling from all directions. The huge field was green with trampled grass that gleamed like lacquer.

Kavalerov watched the box without ever lowering his eyes. He strained to see, and staring, put his imagination to work, trying to catch what he couldn't make out from that distance. He wasn't the only one. Many of those sitting close to the box, even though they were excited by the extraordinary spectacle to come, were drawn to the enchanting young woman in the pink dress, almost a girl, as careless as a child about the way she sat and moved, who at the same time possessed a look that made everyone want to be noticed by her, as if she were a celebrity or the daughter of a famous man.

Twenty thousand spectators crowded the stadium. This would be an unprecedented event—the long-awaited match between the teams of Moscow and Germany.

In the stands people were arguing, shouting, picking fights. The stadium was bursting with all the people. Somewhere a railing broke with a ducklike cry. Kavalerov, tangled up in other people's knees and in search of his own seat, saw a distinguished old man in a cream-colored vest lying on the track at the foot of the stands, breathing heavily, his arms thrown back. People were winding their way past him, giving him little thought. His alarm was intensified by the wind. Flags beat against the towers like lightning.

Kavalerov's entire being strained toward the box. Valya was seated above him, catercorner, about twenty meters away. His vision was playing tricks on him. He thought their eyes met. Then he half rose. He thought he saw a medal flash on her. The wind was having its way with her. From time to time she grabbed onto her hat. It was a bonnet made of shiny red straw. The wind was blowing her sleeve all the way up to her shoulder, baring her arm, which was as slender as a flute. A poster flapped its wings, flew away from her, and fell into the thick of things.

As much as a month before the match people had been assuming that the German team would bring the famous Goetske, who played center forward, that is, the principal player of the five attackers. And indeed, Goetske had come. As soon as the German team came onto the field to the strains of a march and before the players could spread out over the field, the public (as always happens) recognized the celebrity, even though the celebrity was walking with the other visitors.

"Goetske! Goetske!" shouted the spectators, experiencing a special pleasure at the sight of the famous player and clapping for him.

Goetske, who turned out to be a short, swarthy-faced, round-shouldered little man, stepped off to one side, stopped, raised his arms over his head, and shook his clasped hands. This novel foreign greeting thrilled the spectators even more.

The group of Germans, in their vivid, richly colored clothes—about eleven of them—positively shone on the green, in the purity of the air. They were wearing tan, almost golden, jerseys with green stripes down the right side of the chest and black shorts. Their shorts were flapping in the wind.

Volodya Makarov, shrinking from the freshness of his

newly donned soccer shirt, looked out the window of the soccer players' building. The Germans had reached the middle of the field.

"Shall we go?" he asked. "Shall we?"

"Let's go!" the team captain commanded.

The Soviet team ran out in their red shirts and white shorts. The spectators were draped over the railings, stamping their feet on the boards. The roar drowned out the music.

The Germans had to play the first half of the game with their backs to the wind.

Our team not only played and tried to do everything they could to play their best, but also never stopped being spectators, watching the Germans' play, or professionals, assessing their game. The game lasted ninety minutes, with a short break at the forty-fifth minute. After the break the teams would switch halves of the field. Given the windy weather, it was more advantageous to play into the wind when you were fresh.

Since the Germans were playing with the wind and the wind was very strong, all through the game the ball kept blowing toward our goal. It almost never left the Soviet end of the field. Our backs kicked strong "candles," that is, high parabolic kicks, but the ball, skidding along the wall of wind, would spin around, shiny yellow, and find its way back. The Germans were attacking ferociously. The famous Goetske turned out to be a dangerous player, indeed. All eyes were riveted on him.

When Goetske got the ball, Valya, sitting up top, would scream, as if she were about to see something horrible and criminal any second now. Goetske broke through to the goal, leaving our backs laid flat by his speed and force, and kicked it at the goal. Then Valya, swaying toward her neighbor, grabbed her neighbor's hand in both of hers, pressed her cheek to it, and thinking only of one thing—hiding her face and not seeing the horrible thing—continued to watch through squinting eyes the terrifying movements of Goetske, who was black from running in the heat.

But Volodya Makarov, goalkeeper for the Soviet team, caught the ball. Before he could finish his kick, Goetske elegantly exchanged this motion for another one he needed in order to turn around and run, so he turned and ran, bending his back, which was tightly swathed by the jersey black with sweat. Valya immediately resumed her natural pose and started laughing—first from relief that they hadn't kicked the ball in against our side, and second because she remembered how she'd been screaming and grabbing her neighbor's hand.

"Makarov! Makarov! Bravo, Makarov!" she shouted along with everyone.

Every minute the ball was flying toward the goal. It struck the goalposts, they moaned, and lime sprinkled off them... Volodya would catch the ball in midflight, when it seemed mathematically impossible. The entire audience, the entire living slope of the stands seemed to get steeper; each spectator was halfway to his feet, impelled by a terrible, impatient desire to see, at last, the most interesting thing—the scoring of a goal. The referees were sticking whistles into their lips as they walked, ready to whistle for a goal...Volodya wasn't catching the ball, he was ripping it from its line of flight, like someone who has violated the laws of physics and was hit by the stunning action of thwarted forces. He would fly up with the ball, spinning around, literally screwing himself up on it. He would grab the ball with his entire body—knees, belly, and chin—throwing his weight at the speed of the ball, the way someone throws a rag down to put out a flame. The usurped speed of the ball would throw Volodya two meters to the side, and he would fall like a firecracker. The opposing forwards would run at him, but ultimately the ball would end up high above the fray.

Volodya stayed inside the goal. He couldn't just stand there, though. He walked the line of the goal from post to post, trying to tamp down the surge of energy from his battle with the ball. Everything was roaring inside him. He swung his arms, shook himself, kicked up a clump of earth with his toe. Elegant before the start of the game, he now consisted of rags, a black body, and the leather of his huge, fingerless gloves. The breaks didn't last long. Once again the Germans' attack would roll toward Moscow's goal. Volodya passionately desired victory for his team and worried about each of his players. He thought that only he knew how you should play against Goetske, what his weak points were, how to defend against his attacks. He was also interested in what opinion the famous German was forming about the Soviet game. When he himself clapped and shouted "hurray" to each of his backs, he felt like shouting to Goetske then: "Look how we're playing! Do you think we're playing well?"

As a soccer player, Volodya was Goetske's exact opposite. Volodya was a professional athlete; the other was a professional player. What was important to Volodya was the overall progress of the game, the overall victory, the outcome; Goetske was anxious merely to demonstrate his art. He was an old hand who was not there to support the team's honor; he treasured only his own success; he was not a permanent member of any sports organization because he had compromised himself by moving from club to club for money. He was barred from participating in play-off matches. He was invited only for friendly games, exhibition games, and trips to other countries. He combined art and luck. His presence made a team dangerous. He despised the other players—both his side and his opponents. He knew he could kick a goal against any team. The rest didn't matter to him. He was a hack.

By the middle of the game it was clear to the spectators that the Soviet team was not giving in to the Germans. They couldn't carry off a proper attack. Goetske was preventing it. He was a spoiler, wrecking their plays. He was playing only for himself, at his own risk, neither taking nor giving help. When he got the ball, he drew all the play to himself, squeezed it into a lump, let go, and struck it, switching from one side of the field to the other—according to his own plans, which were unclear to his partners, relying only on himself, on his running and his ability to get around his opponent.

From this the spectators concluded that the second half of the game, when Goetske would run out of breath and ours would get the wind at their backs, would end in a rout of the Germans. If only ours could hold on now and not let a single ball into the goal.

But this time the virtuoso Goetske prevailed. Ten minutes before the end of the first half he broke right, brought the ball along with his torso, then stopped short, cutting off the pursuit which, not expecting him to stop, ran ahead and to the right. He turned with the ball toward the center and crossed an open space, getting around just one Soviet back, and drove the ball straight at the goal, glancing back and forth at his feet and then at the goal, as if estimating and calculating the speed, direction, and timing of the kick.

A solid wailing "o-o-o" rolled from the stands.

Volodya, squatting and spreading his arms out as if he were holding an invisible barrel, readied himself to grab the ball. But Goetske didn't kick, he ran up to the goal. Volodya fell at his feet. The ball got stuck between the two men, like in a barrel; then the spectators' whistles and stamping covered the scene's finale. From the kick of one of the men the ball flew up lightly and shakily over Goetske's head, and he drove it into the net with a strike of his head that looked like a bow.

The Soviet team was a goal down.

The stadium roared. Binoculars turned in the direction of the Soviet goal. Goetske, looking at his flashing shoes, ran pretentiously toward the middle.

Volodya's comrades picked him up.

9

VALYA turned along with everyone else. Kavalerov saw her facing him. He had no doubt she saw him. He started to fidget, and a bizarre idea enraged him. He thought the people around him were laughing at him; they'd noticed his anxiety.

He looked at the people sitting next to him. Much to his surprise, sitting in the same row with him, quite nearby, was Andrei Babichev. Once again Kavalerov was indignant at the two white hands adjusting the focus on the binoculars, the large torso in the gray jacket, the trim mustache...

The binoculars loomed over Kavalerov like a black missile. The binocular strap hung from Babichev's cheeks like reins.

The Germans were on the offensive again.

Suddenly the ball, thrown by someone's powerful and miscalculated kick, flew high up and to the side, out of the playing field and in Kavalerov's direction, whistled over the craning heads of the lower rows, hung there for a moment, rotated all its planes, and fell to the boards at Kavalerov's feet. The game came to a standstill. The players stopped, caught by surprise. All at once the picture on the field, green and colorful, in constant motion, froze. The way a movie stops abruptly when the film breaks, when the light has already been turned on in the hall but the technician still hasn't turned the projector light off and the audience sees the strangely whitened frame and the outlines of the hero frozen in a pose that speaks of the most rapid movement. Kavalerov's hatred intensified. Everyone around him was laughing. A ball landing in the rows always makes people laugh: at that moment the spectators seem to realize the true silliness of men running after a ball for an hour and a half, compelling them—the spectators, the bystanders—to view their utterly frivolous time wasting with such gravity and passion.

At that moment, all the thousands did their utmost to give Kavalerov their unwanted attention, and this attention was easily entertained.

Even Valya may have been laughing at him, the man the ball had landed in front of! She may have been laughing twice as hard, making fun of her enemy's ridiculous position. He smirked, edging his foot away from the ball, which, losing its support, bumped up against his heel with feline attachment.

"Well!" exclaimed Babichev, unhappy and surprised. Kavalerov was passive. Two large white hands reached for the ball. Someone picked up the ball and handed it to Babichev. He rose to his full height, and thrusting his belly out, drew his arms holding the ball behind his head, swinging the ball so he could throw it farther. He couldn't be serious doing something like this, but realizing that he needed to be serious, he exaggerated his outward expression of gravity, knitting his brows and puffing out his fresh red lips.

Swinging forward hard, Babichev threw the ball, which magically unchained the field.

"He refused to recognize me," Kavalerov fed his hatred.

The first half of the game ended with the German team ahead by one to nothing... The players, with dark bruises on their faces and green blades of grass stuck to them, were walking toward the passageway, moving their bare knees powerfully and broadly, like in water. The Germans, who were red in a not very Russian way, with a flush that began at their temples, mixed in colorfully with the Muscovites. The players were walking, seeing everyone en masse—the whole crowd under the wooden walls of the passageway—and no one individually. They smeared the crowd with smiles and lifeless eyes that were too transparent on their darkened faces. Those who had just seen them as tiny multicolored little figures, running and falling, now saw them face-to-face. The noise of the game, which had yet to subside, traveled with them. Goetske, who looked like a gypsy, was walking, sucking at the cut he'd just received above his elbow.

The news for the gawkers was the players' height and build, the severity of the scratches, their heavy breathing and complete disarray. From far away it all made a much flimsier, more transparent impression.

Kavalerov squeezed between strangers and under a crossbeam, stepping with relief onto the grass. Here, in the shadow, he ran with others down the path, circling around behind the stands. The refreshment area set out on the lawn under the trees filled up in an instant. The crumpled little old man in the cream-colored vest, still glancing at the public unhappily and warily, was eating ice cream. The crowd was crawling toward the field house.

"Hurrah! Makarov! Hurrah!" the ecstatic shouts carried from there. The fans were climbing the fences, fending off the barbed wire as if it were bees—and higher, like forest gnomes: into the trees, into the dark greenery, which swayed from the wind and their agility.

A gleaming body swinging its nakedness soared at a slant over the crowd. They were swinging Volodya Makarov.

Kavalerov didn't have the heart to push into the winner's circle. He peeked through the gaps, shifting from side to side behind the crowd.

Volodya was standing on the ground now. The sock on one foot had fallen and rolled down like a green pretzel around his pear-shaped, slightly hairy ankle. His clawed shirt was barely clinging to his torso. He had wisely crossed his arms at his chest.

And here stood Valya. And Andrei Babichev was with her.

All three were being applauded by the gawkers.

Babichev was looking lovingly at Volodya.

The wind stirred. A striped awning fell to the ground, and all the leaves swayed to the right. The ring of gawkers broke up, the whole picture went blurry, people tried to protect themselves from the dust. Valya got it worse than anyone. Her pink dress, as light as a husk, flew up over her legs, showing Kavalerov its sheerness. The wind blew the dress against her face, and Kavalerov saw the outline of her face in the glow and sheer of the fabric, which had spread out like a fan. Through the dust Kavalerov saw this and how, in trying to catch her dress, she spun around and got tangled up, nearly falling on her side. She was trying to pin down the hem at her knees, to hold it there, but she couldn't, and then, to put a stop to the indecency, she resorted to half measures: with her arms she hugged her overly exposed legs, hiding her knees, hunching over, like a swimmer caught unawares.

Somewhere the referee whistled. A march began. Thus the good-natured confusion came to an end. The second half of the game was about to begin. Volodya hurried off.

"Two goals minimum against the Germans!" squealed a young boy racing past Kavalerov.

Valya continued to battle the wind. In pursuit of her hem, she changed her position ten times and finally found herself close to Kavalerov, a whisper away.

She was standing with her legs planted widely apart. Her hat, which had been thrown off by the wind and caught in flight, she was holding in her hand. Before she could straighten herself out from her leaps, she looked at Kavalerov without seeing him, barely tilting her head of short chestnut hair, which was cut to a sharp angle at her cheeks.

Sunlight slipped over her shoulder, she swayed, and her clavicle flashed like a dagger. This thought lasted a tenth of a second, long enough to make Kavalerov turn cold at the realization that he would have this incurable longing inside him forever, now that he had seen this otherworldly being, so exotic and special. He was overcome by how hopelessly sweet she looked, how crushingly unattainable her purity was, and how invincible her allure—both because she was a young girl and because she was in love with Volodya.

Babichev was waiting for her, his arm extended.

"Valya," said Kavalerov, "I've waited for you all my life. Have pity on me..."

But she didn't hear. She was running, bent low by the wind.

10

THAT NIGHT Kavalerov came home drunk.

He walked down the hall to the sink—for a good long drink. He opened the tap all the way and soaked himself. He left the tap open, the stream blaring. Walking into Anichka's room, he stopped. The light had not been turned out. Bathed in cottony yellow light, the widow was sitting on her huge bed, her bare legs hanging over the side. She was ready for bed.

Kavalerov took a step. She was silent, as if under a spell. Kavalerov thought she was smiling, beckoning.

He went toward her.

She did not resist and even opened her arms.

"Oh you little nuthatch," she whispered. "Look at you, you little nuthatch."

Later he woke up. He'd been torn by thirst, by a drunken, frenzied dream about water. He woke up—and all was quiet. A second before he awoke the piercing memory of the stream gushing in the sink came to him—but there wasn't any water. He drifted off again. While he slept, the widow was keeping house: she turned off the tap, undressed the sleeping man, and mended his suspenders. Morning came. At first Kavalerov didn't know what was what. Like the drunken beggar in the comedy who is taken in by a rich man and brought to his palace, he lay there, hung over, amid unaccustomed luxury. He saw his unprecedented reflection in a mirror—soles front. He lay there magnificently, his arms crossed behind his head. The sun shone on him from the side. It was as if he were hovering in the cupola of a temple, in broad, smoking bands of light. And above him hung bunches of grapes, cupids danced, apples spilled from horns of plenty—and he could almost hear an organ coming from all this. He was lying on Anichka's bed.

"You remind me of him," Anichka whispered hotly, leaning over him.

Above the bed hung a glass-covered portrait. A man, someone's young grandfather, formally dressed—in one of the last frock coats of the era. You could tell: he had a strong, multi-barreled occiput. The man was about fifty-seven.

Kavalerov remembered his father changing his shirt...

"You remind me a lot of my husband," repeated Anichka, embracing Kavalerov. And Kavalerov's head slipped under her arm, as into a tent. The widow opened the tents of her arms. Ecstasy and shame raged inside her.

"He took me like that, too...by cunning...quietly, oh so silently, never said anything...but then! Oh you, my little nuthatch..."

Kavalerov struck her.

She staggered back. Kavalerov jumped from the bed, tearing apart the layers of bedding; the sheets trailing after him. She rushed for the door, her arms pleaded for help, she ran, chased by her goods and chattel, like a woman of Pompeii. A basket collapsed, a chair listed.

He struck her several times on her back and waist, which was ringed with fat, like a tire.

The chair was balancing on one leg.

"He beat me, too," she said, smiling through her tears.

Kavalerov went back to the bed. He collapsed, feeling like he was going to be sick. He lay oblivious the whole day. In the evening, the widow lay down beside him. She snored. Kavalerov pictured her larynx in the shape of an arch leading into the gloom. He was hiding behind the arch's vault. Everything trembled and quivered, and the ground shook. Kavalerov slipped and was knocked down by the air flying from the abyss. The sleeping woman moaned. Once she stopped moaning and fell silent, after smacking her lips noisily. The entire architecture of her larynx was warping. Her snore got powdery, fizzy.

Kavalerov thrashed and cried. She got up and put a wet towel on his forehead. He leaned toward the wetness, lifting his whole body, searched for the towel with his hands, bunched it up, pressing it to his cheek, and kissed it, whispering, "They stole her from me... Living in this world is so hard... So hard..."

But the widow had barely lain down before she had fallen asleep, perching close to the mirror arch. Sleep smeared her with sweetness. She slept with her mouth open, gurgling, the way old women sleep.

There were bedbugs, and they rustled as if someone were lashing the wallpaper. There were bedbug hiding places of which the day knew nothing. The bed-tree grew and swelled.

The windowsill turned pink.

Gloom gathered around the bed. The night's secrets dropped down the walls from the corners, flowed over the sleeping pair, and crawled under the bed.

Kavalerov suddenly sat up, his eyes wide open.

Over the bed stood Ivan.

11

KAVALEROV started packing right away.

Anichka was sleeping in a sitting position under the arch, her hands clasped over her belly. Cautiously, so as not to disturb her, he pulled off the blanket, and, donning it like a cloak, stood before Ivan.

"Well, this is excellent," said the other. "You're twinkling like a lizard. That's what you should look like when you appear before the people. Let's go, let's go. We have to hurry."

"I'm very sick," Kavalerov sighed. He smiled meekly, as if apologizing for the fact that he had no desire to look for his trousers, jacket, and shoes. "Does it matter that I'm barefoot?"

Ivan was already in the hall. Kavalerov hurried after him.

"I've been suffering for a long time for no reason," thought Kavalerov. "This is payback day."

They got caught up in the stream of people. Past the next corner a gleaming road came into view.

"There it is!" said Ivan, squeezing Kavalerov's arm. "There's the Two Bits!"

Kavalerov saw it: gardens, spherical clumps of leaves, an arch made of light translucent stone, galleries, a ball flying above the greenery...

"Over here!" Ivan commanded.

They ran along the wall, which was covered in ivy, then had to jump. The blue blanket made the jump easier for Kavalerov, he flew through the air and over the crowd and landed at the foot of a very broad stone staircase. Immediately, frightened, he began crawling away under his blanket, like an insect folding its wings. No one noticed him. He crouched behind a pedestal.

At the top of the stairs, surrounded by young people, stood Andrei Babichev. He stood there with his arm around Volodya.

"They're just about to bring her in," said Andrei, smiling at his friends.

And at that Kavalerov saw the following: down the asphalt road leading to the steps of the staircase came an orchestra, and soaring above the orchestra was Valya. The sound of the instruments was holding her up. She was being borne along by the sound. She would ascend and descend above the brass depending on the height and force of the sound. Her ribbons were flying higher than their heads, her dress was billowing, her hair was swept upward.

The final passage dropped her at the top of the stairs, and she fell into Volodya's arms. Everyone stepped back. Those two remained in the circle.

Kavalerov didn't see what came next. A sudden horror gripped him. A strange shadow suddenly moved in front of him. Freezing, he slowly turned around. On the grass, a pace behind him, sat Ophelia.

"A-a-agh!" he began shouting terribly. He hurried to escape. Ophelia jingled and grabbed him by the blanket. It slid off. In his shameful state of undress, stumbling, falling, striking his jaw on the stone, he scrambled up the staircase. The others were looking up. The lovely Valya stood there, stooping.

"Ophelia, back!" Ivan's voice rang out. "She's not obeying me . . . Ophelia, stop!"

"Hold her!"

"She's going to kill him!"

"Oh!"

"Watch out! Watch out!"

Kavalerov looked back from halfway up the staircase. Ivan was trying to scramble up the wall. The ivy pulled away. The crowd surged back. Ivan was hanging on the wall from arms set wide apart. The frightening iron thing was moving slowly across the grass in his direction. Out of what might be called the thing's head a gleaming needle was slowly poking through. Ivan howled. He was losing his grip. He fell, his bowler rolled away among the dandelions. He sat, his back pressed to the wall, his hands covering his face. The machine kept advancing, tearing dandelions as it went.

Kavalerov got up and in a voice full of despair began to shout, "Save him! Would you really let a machine kill a man?"

No answer followed.

"My place is with him!" said Kavalerov. "Teacher! I shall die with you!"

But it was too late. Ivan's cowardly wail made him collapse. As he fell, he saw Ivan skewered to the wall.

Ivan tilted quietly, turning on the terrible axis.

Kavalerov buried his head in his arms, so as not to see or hear anything more. Still he heard the clanking. The machine was mounting the stairs.

"I don't want to die!" he shouted with all his might. "She's going to kill me! Forgive me! Forgive me! Spare me! I wasn't the one who defamed the machine! I'm not to blame. Valya! Valya! Save me!"

12

KAVALEROV was sick for three days. Once he recovered, he tried to escape.

He climbed down, staring at a single point: the floor by the corner of the bed. He dressed like an automaton and suddenly felt a new leather loop on his suspenders. The widow had done away with his safety pin. Where had she gotten the loop? Had she taken it off her husband's old suspenders? Kavalerov fully realized the vileness of his situation. He ran into the hall jacketless. He detached the red suspenders as he went and tossed them aside.

He hesitated on the threshold of the landing. There were no voices coming from the yard. Then he stepped onto the landing, and all his thoughts became confused. The sweetest sensations arose—yearning, joy. It was a lovely morning. There was a light breeze (that seemed to be turning the pages of a book) and the sky was blue. Kavalerov was standing over a befouled spot. A cat, frightened by his sudden movement, ran out of the trash bin; some kind of filth fluttered down after her. What could be poetic in a pigsty enveloped in so many curses? He stood there craning his neck and stretching his arms.

At that moment he felt the time had come, the line had been drawn between two existences—the time for a catastrophe!—the time to break, break with everything that had been . . . right now, this minute, and in two heartbeats, no more; he had to cross that line, and life, repugnant, chaotic, not his—alien, violent life—would be left behind . . .

He stood there, eyes wide open, and from his running and agitation and because he was still weak, his entire field of vision pulsed before him and turned pink.

He realized how far he had fallen. It had been inevitable. He had lived too easy and conceited a life, he had held too high an opinion of himself. He was a lazy, foul, and capricious man.

Kavalerov understood everything as he flew over the sty.

He went back, collected his suspenders, and dressed. A spoon clanked—the widow was reaching out for him—but he left the building without looking back. Once again he spent the night on the boulevard. And once again he returned. But he made a firm decision: "I'll put the widow in her place. I won't let her so much as hiccup about what happened. Lots can happen when there's drinking involved. But I can't live on the street."

The widow was lighting a small piece of kindling over the burner. She looked at him sideways and smiled smugly. He walked into the room. Hanging on the corner of the cupboard was Ivan's bowler.

Ivan was sitting on the bed, looking like his brother, only smaller. A blanket surrounded him like a cloud. On the table was a wine bottle. Ivan was sipping from a glass of red wine. Evidently he had just woken up: his face hadn't smoothed out yet, and he was still scratching dreamily somewhere under the blanket.

"What does this mean?" Kavalerov asked the classic question.

Ivan smiled clearly.

"This means, my friend, that we need a drink. Anichka, a glass!"

Anichka came in. She searched in the cupboard.

"Don't be jealous, Kolya," she said, hugging Kavalerov. "He's very lonely, just like you. I pity you both."

"What does this mean?" Kavalerov asked softly.

YURI OLESHA

"Why harp on that?" Ivan got angry. "It doesn't mean anything."

He climbed off the bed, holding on to his drawers, and poured Kavalerov some wine.

"Let's drink, Kavalerov...We've talked a lot about emotions...And we forgot the main one, my friend...We forgot indifference...Didn't we? In fact...I think that indifference is the best of all conditions of the human mind. Let's be indifferent, Kavalerov. Take a look! We've got ourselves a room, my friend. Drink. To indifference. Hurrah! To Anichka! And today, by the way...listen: I've got some good news for you...Today, Kavalerov, is your turn to sleep with Anichka. Hurrah!"

Moscow
February–June 1927

TITLES IN SERIES

For a complete list of titles, visit www.nyrb.com or write to:
Catalog Requests, NYRB, 435 Hudson Street, New York, NY 10014

J.R. ACKERLEY Hindoo Holiday*
J.R. ACKERLEY My Dog Tulip*
J.R. ACKERLEY My Father and Myself*
J.R. ACKERLEY We Think the World of You*
HENRY ADAMS The Jeffersonian Transformation
CÉLESTE ALBARET Monsieur Proust
DANTE ALIGHIERI The Inferno
DANTE ALIGHIERI The New Life
WILLIAM ATTAWAY Blood on the Forge
W.H. AUDEN (EDITOR) The Living Thoughts of Kierkegaard
W.H. AUDEN W.H. Auden's Book of Light Verse
ERICH AUERBACH Dante: Poet of the Secular World
DOROTHY BAKER Cassandra at the Wedding
J.A. BAKER The Peregrine
HONORÉ DE BALZAC The Unknown Masterpiece *and* Gambara*
MAX BEERBOHM Seven Men
STEPHEN BENATAR Wish Her Safe at Home*
FRANS G. BENGTSSON The Long Ships*
ALEXANDER BERKMAN Prison Memoirs of an Anarchist
GEORGES BERNANOS Mouchette
ADOLFO BIOY CASARES Asleep in the Sun
ADOLFO BIOY CASARES The Invention of Morel
CAROLINE BLACKWOOD Corrigan*
CAROLINE BLACKWOOD Great Granny Webster*
NICOLAS BOUVIER The Way of the World
MALCOLM BRALY On the Yard*
MILLEN BRAND The Outward Room*
JOHN HORNE BURNS The Gallery
ROBERT BURTON The Anatomy of Melancholy
CAMARA LAYE The Radiance of the King
GIROLAMO CARDANO The Book of My Life
DON CARPENTER Hard Rain Falling*
J.L. CARR A Month in the Country
BLAISE CENDRARS Moravagine
EILEEN CHANG Love in a Fallen City
UPAMANYU CHATTERJEE English, August: An Indian Story
NIRAD C. CHAUDHURI The Autobiography of an Unknown Indian
ANTON CHEKHOV Peasants and Other Stories
RICHARD COBB Paris and Elsewhere
COLETTE The Pure and the Impure
JOHN COLLIER Fancies and Goodnights
CARLO COLLODI The Adventures of Pinocchio*
IVY COMPTON-BURNETT A House and Its Head
IVY COMPTON-BURNETT Manservant and Maidservant
BARBARA COMYNS The Vet's Daughter
EVAN S. CONNELL The Diary of a Rapist
ALBERT COSSERY The Jokers*
ALBERT COSSERY Proud Beggars*

* *Also available as an electronic book.*

HAROLD CRUSE The Crisis of the Negro Intellectual
ASTOLPHE DE CUSTINE Letters from Russia
LORENZO DA PONTE Memoirs
ELIZABETH DAVID A Book of Mediterranean Food
ELIZABETH DAVID Summer Cooking
L.J. DAVIS A Meaningful Life*
VIVANT DENON No Tomorrow/Point de lendemain
MARIA DERMOÛT The Ten Thousand Things
DER NISTER The Family Mashber
TIBOR DÉRY Niki: The Story of a Dog
ARTHUR CONAN DOYLE The Exploits and Adventures of Brigadier Gerard
CHARLES DUFF A Handbook on Hanging
BRUCE DUFFY The World As I Found It*
DAPHNE DU MAURIER Don't Look Now: Stories
ELAINE DUNDY The Dud Avocado*
ELAINE DUNDY The Old Man and Me*
G.B. EDWARDS The Book of Ebenezer Le Page
MARCELLUS EMANTS A Posthumous Confession
EURIPIDES Grief Lessons: Four Plays; translated by Anne Carson
J.G. FARRELL Troubles*
J.G. FARRELL The Siege of Krishnapur*
J.G. FARRELL The Singapore Grip*
ELIZA FAY Original Letters from India
KENNETH FEARING The Big Clock
KENNETH FEARING Clark Gifford's Body
FÉLIX FÉNÉON Novels in Three Lines*
M.I. FINLEY The World of Odysseus
THEODOR FONTANE Irretrievable*
EDWIN FRANK (EDITOR) Unknown Masterpieces
MASANOBU FUKUOKA The One-Straw Revolution*
MARC FUMAROLI When the World Spoke French
CARLO EMILIO GADDA That Awful Mess on the Via Merulana
MAVIS GALLANT The Cost of Living: Early and Uncollected Stories*
MAVIS GALLANT Paris Stories*
MAVIS GALLANT Varieties of Exile*
GABRIEL GARCÍA MÁRQUEZ Clandestine in Chile: The Adventures of Miguel Littín
ALAN GARNER Red Shift*
THÉOPHILE GAUTIER My Fantoms
JEAN GENET Prisoner of Love
ÉLISABETH GILLE The Mirador: Dreamed Memories of Irène Némirovsky by Her Daughter*
JOHN GLASSCO Memoirs of Montparnasse*
P.V. GLOB The Bog People: Iron-Age Man Preserved
EDMOND AND JULES DE GONCOURT Pages from the Goncourt Journals
EDWARD GOREY (EDITOR) The Haunted Looking Glass
A.C. GRAHAM Poems of the Late T'ang
WILLIAM LINDSAY GRESHAM Nightmare Alley*
EMMETT GROGAN Ringolevio: A Life Played for Keeps
VASILY GROSSMAN Everything Flows*
VASILY GROSSMAN Life and Fate*
VASILY GROSSMAN The Road*
OAKLEY HALL Warlock
PATRICK HAMILTON The Slaves of Solitude
PATRICK HAMILTON Twenty Thousand Streets Under the Sky

PETER HANDKE Short Letter, Long Farewell

PETER HANDKE Slow Homecoming

ELIZABETH HARDWICK The New York Stories of Elizabeth Hardwick*

ELIZABETH HARDWICK Seduction and Betrayal*

ELIZABETH HARDWICK Sleepless Nights*

L.P. HARTLEY Eustace and Hilda: A Trilogy*

L.P. HARTLEY The Go-Between*

NATHANIEL HAWTHORNE Twenty Days with Julian & Little Bunny by Papa

GILBERT HIGHET Poets in a Landscape

JANET HOBHOUSE The Furies

HUGO VON HOFMANNSTHAL The Lord Chandos Letter

JAMES HOGG The Private Memoirs and Confessions of a Justified Sinner

RICHARD HOLMES Shelley: The Pursuit

ALISTAIR HORNE A Savage War of Peace: Algeria 1954–1962*

GEOFFREY HOUSEHOLD Rogue Male*

WILLIAM DEAN HOWELLS Indian Summer

BOHUMIL HRABAL Dancing Lessons for the Advanced in Age*

RICHARD HUGHES A High Wind in Jamaica*

RICHARD HUGHES In Hazard

RICHARD HUGHES The Fox in the Attic (The Human Predicament, Vol. 1)

RICHARD HUGHES The Wooden Shepherdess (The Human Predicament, Vol. 2)

MAUDE HUTCHINS Victorine

YASUSHI INOUE Tun-huang*

HENRY JAMES The Ivory Tower

HENRY JAMES The New York Stories of Henry James*

HENRY JAMES The Other House

HENRY JAMES The Outcry

TOVE JANSSON Fair Play

TOVE JANSSON The Summer Book

TOVE JANSSON The True Deceiver

RANDALL JARRELL (EDITOR) Randall Jarrell's Book of Stories

DAVID JONES In Parenthesis

KABIR Songs of Kabir; translated by Arvind Krishna Mehrotra*

FRIGYES KARINTHY A Journey Round My Skull

HELEN KELLER The World I Live In

YASHAR KEMAL Memed, My Hawk

YASHAR KEMAL They Burn the Thistles

MURRAY KEMPTON Part of Our Time: Some Ruins and Monuments of the Thirties

DAVID KIDD Peking Story*

ROBERT KIRK The Secret Commonwealth of Elves, Fauns, and Fairies

ARUN KOLATKAR Jejuri

DEZSŐ KOSZTOLÁNYI Skylark*

TÉTÉ-MICHEL KPOMASSIE An African in Greenland

GYULA KRÚDY The Adventures of Sindbad*

GYULA KRÚDY Sunflower*

SIGIZMUND KRZHIZHANOVSKY The Letter Killers Club*

SIGIZMUND KRZHIZHANOVSKY Memories of the Future

MARGARET LEECH Reveille in Washington: 1860–1865*

PATRICK LEIGH FERMOR Between the Woods and the Water*

PATRICK LEIGH FERMOR Mani: Travels in the Southern Peloponnese*

PATRICK LEIGH FERMOR Roumeli: Travels in Northern Greece*

PATRICK LEIGH FERMOR A Time of Gifts*

PATRICK LEIGH FERMOR A Time to Keep Silence*

PATRICK LEIGH FERMOR The Traveller's Tree*

D.B. WYNDHAM LEWIS AND CHARLES LEE (EDITORS) The Stuffed Owl

GEORG CHRISTOPH LICHTENBERG The Waste Books

JAKOV LIND Soul of Wood and Other Stories

H.P. LOVECRAFT AND OTHERS The Colour Out of Space

DWIGHT MACDONALD Masscult and Midcult: Essays Against the American Grain*

NORMAN MAILER Miami and the Siege of Chicago*

JANET MALCOLM In the Freud Archives

JEAN-PATRICK MANCHETTE Fatale*

OSIP MANDELSTAM The Selected Poems of Osip Mandelstam

OLIVIA MANNING Fortunes of War: The Balkan Trilogy

OLIVIA MANNING School for Love*

JAMES VANCE MARSHALL Walkabout*

GUY DE MAUPASSANT Afloat

GUY DE MAUPASSANT Alien Hearts*

JAMES MCCOURT Mawrdew Czgowchwz*

HENRI MICHAUX Miserable Miracle

JESSICA MITFORD Hons and Rebels

JESSICA MITFORD Poison Penmanship*

NANCY MITFORD Madame de Pompadour*

HENRY DE MONTHERLANT Chaos and Night

BRIAN MOORE The Lonely Passion of Judith Hearne*

BRIAN MOORE The Mangan Inheritance*

ALBERTO MORAVIA Boredom*

ALBERTO MORAVIA Contempt*

JAN MORRIS Conundrum

JAN MORRIS Hav*

PENELOPE MORTIMER The Pumpkin Eater*

ÁLVARO MUTIS The Adventures and Misadventures of Maqroll

L.H. MYERS The Root and the Flower*

NESCIO Amsterdam Stories*

DARCY O'BRIEN A Way of Life, Like Any Other

YURI OLESHA Envy*

IONA AND PETER OPIE The Lore and Language of Schoolchildren

IRIS OWENS After Claude*

RUSSELL PAGE The Education of a Gardener

ALEXANDROS PAPADIAMANTIS The Murderess

BORIS PASTERNAK, MARINA TSVETAYEVA, AND RAINER MARIA RILKE Letters, Summer 1926

CESARE PAVESE The Moon and the Bonfires

CESARE PAVESE The Selected Works of Cesare Pavese

LUIGI PIRANDELLO The Late Mattia Pascal

ANDREY PLATONOV The Foundation Pit

ANDREY PLATONOV Soul and Other Stories

J.F. POWERS Morte d'Urban

J.F. POWERS The Stories of J.F. Powers

J.F. POWERS Wheat That Springeth Green

CHRISTOPHER PRIEST Inverted World

BOLESŁAW PRUS The Doll*

RAYMOND QUENEAU We Always Treat Women Too Well

RAYMOND QUENEAU Witch Grass

RAYMOND RADIGUET Count d'Orgel's Ball

JULES RENARD Nature Stories*

JEAN RENOIR Renoir, My Father

GREGOR VON REZZORI An Ermine in Czernopol*

GREGOR VON REZZORI Memoirs of an Anti-Semite*

GREGOR VON REZZORI The Snows of Yesteryear: Portraits for an Autobiography*

TIM ROBINSON Stones of Aran: Labyrinth

TIM ROBINSON Stones of Aran: Pilgrimage

MILTON ROKEACH The Three Christs of Ypsilanti*

FR. ROLFE Hadrian the Seventh

GILLIAN ROSE Love's Work

WILLIAM ROUGHEAD Classic Crimes

CONSTANCE ROURKE American Humor: A Study of the National Character

TAYEB SALIH Season of Migration to the North

TAYEB SALIH The Wedding of Zein*

GERSHOM SCHOLEM Walter Benjamin: The Story of a Friendship

DANIEL PAUL SCHREBER Memoirs of My Nervous Illness

JAMES SCHUYLER Alfred and Guinevere

JAMES SCHUYLER What's for Dinner?*

LEONARDO SCIASCIA The Day of the Owl

LEONARDO SCIASCIA Equal Danger

LEONARDO SCIASCIA The Moro Affair

LEONARDO SCIASCIA To Each His Own

LEONARDO SCIASCIA The Wine-Dark Sea

VICTOR SEGALEN René Leys

PHILIPE-PAUL DE SÉGUR Defeat: Napoleon's Russian Campaign

VICTOR SERGE The Case of Comrade Tulayev*

VICTOR SERGE Conquered City*

VICTOR SERGE Unforgiving Years

SHCHEDRIN The Golovlyov Family

GEORGES SIMENON Act of Passion*

GEORGES SIMENON Dirty Snow*

GEORGES SIMENON The Engagement

GEORGES SIMENON The Man Who Watched Trains Go By

GEORGES SIMENON Monsieur Monde Vanishes*

GEORGES SIMENON Pedigree*

GEORGES SIMENON Red Lights

GEORGES SIMENON The Strangers in the House

GEORGES SIMENON Three Bedrooms in Manhattan*

GEORGES SIMENON Tropic Moon*

GEORGES SIMENON The Widow*

CHARLES SIMIC Dime-Store Alchemy: The Art of Joseph Cornell

MAY SINCLAIR Mary Olivier: A Life*

TESS SLESINGER The Unpossessed: A Novel of the Thirties

VLADIMIR SOROKIN Ice Trilogy*

VLADIMIR SOROKIN The Queue

DAVID STACTON The Judges of the Secret Court*

JEAN STAFFORD The Mountain Lion

CHRISTINA STEAD Letty Fox: Her Luck

GEORGE R. STEWART Names on the Land

STENDHAL The Life of Henry Brulard

ADALBERT STIFTER Rock Crystal

THEODOR STORM The Rider on the White Horse

JEAN STROUSE Alice James: A Biography*

HOWARD STURGIS Belchamber

ITALO SVEVO As a Man Grows Older

HARVEY SWADOS Nights in the Gardens of Brooklyn
A.J.A. SYMONS The Quest for Corvo
ELIZABETH TAYLOR Angel*
ELIZABETH TAYLOR A Game of Hide and Seek*
HENRY DAVID THOREAU The Journal: 1837–1861*
TATYANA TOLSTAYA The Slynx
TATYANA TOLSTAYA White Walls: Collected Stories
EDWARD JOHN TRELAWNY Records of Shelley, Byron, and the Author
LIONEL TRILLING The Liberal Imagination
LIONEL TRILLING The Middle of the Journey
IVAN TURGENEV Virgin Soil
JULES VALLÈS The Child
MARK VAN DOREN Shakespeare
CARL VAN VECHTEN The Tiger in the House
ELIZABETH VON ARNIM The Enchanted April*
EDWARD LEWIS WALLANT The Tenants of Moonbloom
ROBERT WALSER Berlin Stories*
ROBERT WALSER Jakob von Gunten
REX WARNER Men and Gods
SYLVIA TOWNSEND WARNER Lolly Willowes*
SYLVIA TOWNSEND WARNER Mr. Fortune*
SYLVIA TOWNSEND WARNER Summer Will Show*
ALEKSANDER WAT My Century
C.V. WEDGWOOD The Thirty Years War
SIMONE WEIL AND RACHEL BESPALOFF War and the Iliad
GLENWAY WESCOTT Apartment in Athens*
GLENWAY WESCOTT The Pilgrim Hawk*
REBECCA WEST The Fountain Overflows
EDITH WHARTON The New York Stories of Edith Wharton*
PATRICK WHITE Riders in the Chariot
T.H. WHITE The Goshawk
JOHN WILLIAMS Butcher's Crossing*
JOHN WILLIAMS Stoner*
ANGUS WILSON Anglo-Saxon Attitudes
EDMUND WILSON Memoirs of Hecate County
RUDOLF AND MARGARET WITTKOWER Born Under Saturn
GEOFFREY WOLFF Black Sun*
FRANCIS WYNDHAM The Complete Fiction
JOHN WYNDHAM The Chrysalids
STEFAN ZWEIG Beware of Pity*
STEFAN ZWEIG Chess Story*
STEFAN ZWEIG Journey Into the Past
STEFAN ZWEIG The Post-Office Girl